The Word of God: Jesus Christ

By

C. Jack Brinkman

xulon
PRESS

ISBN-13: 978-1-59160-726-7
ISBN-10: 1-591607-26-4

Library of Congress Control Number: 2003091986

www.xulonpress.com

Contents

v

Nihil Obstat

"The Word of God: Jesus Christ"
1st Edition
By C. Jack Brinkman

Msgr. John P. Zenz
Censor Deputatus

Dated: September 13, 2002

IMPRIMATUR

Adam Cardinal Maida
Archbishop of Detroit

Dated: September 13, 2002

Nihil Obstat

"The Word of God: Jesus Christ"
2nd Edition
By C. Jack Brinkman

Msgr. John P. Zenz
Censor Deputatus

Dated: January 16, 2004

IMPRIMATUR

Adam Cardinal Maida
Archbishop of Detroit

Dated: January 16, 2004

LETTER FROM THE VATICAN

From the Vatican, August 23, 2003

SECRETARIAT OF STATE

FIRST SECTION – GENERAL AFFAIRS

Dear Mr. Brinkman,

The Holy Father wishes me to express his gratitude for your kind Letter and the gift of your book, *The Word of God: Jesus Christ*. He very much appreciates your thoughtful gesture.

His Holiness will remember your intentions in his prayers. Invoking upon you and your family God's blessings of joy and peace, he Cordially imparts his Apostolic Blessing.

Sincerely yours,

Monsignor Tommaso Caputo
Chief of Protocol

SECRETARIAT OF STATE
First Section-General Affairs

From the Vataican,20July 2006

The Secretariat of State is directed by His Holiness Pope Benedict XV! To acknowledge the book sent to him by C. Jack Brinkman.

The Secretariat of State also has the honor to express His Holiness's appreciation of the respectful sentiments which prompted this presentation.

signed by
Monsignor Gabriele Caccia
Assessor

Dedication

This little book, THE WORD OF GOD: JESUS CHRIST, is dedicated to my three women. With my first woman, my mother, I experienced real, constant, unselfish, memorable, and maternal love.

With my second woman, my wife with whom I have enjoyed over 50 years of happy Sacramental Marriage, I experienced and know real, constant, unselfish, memorable, romantic, and spousal love.

With my third woman, Mary the Mother of Jesus, my spiritual mother, she was given to me over twenty hundred years ago, when Jesus said to the disciple, John, "She is your mother (John 19:27)." She is the spiritual mother of all who love her son Jesus. Yet in some of her apparitions she described herself as the spiritual mother of all humans with the hope that even those who do not love her Son, will convert and begin to recognize and love her Son Jesus Christ. I have experienced real, constant, unselfish, memorable, spiritual love from Mary when she conditions me to know, love and serve her son Jesus, the Son of God and as God who became human. She has interceded for me in my prayers. "I urge that petitions, prayers, requests, and thanksgivings be offered to God for all people (1 Timothy 2:1)." As I have made intercessory prayers for others, she has certainly made intercessory prayers for me, with and sometimes without my request I have even experienced a suspension of the laws of nature with her intercessory prayers for me..

Introduction

As a Catholic for over 75 years, I have experienced a profound deepening of my faith through the Bible. My Bible studies began while in the Air Force during peace time. I considered myself a good Catholic prior to getting into scripture. Yet with serious Bible study, I have acquired a 'road map' for life. With faith in God's word, I have confidently applied Pr 16:9. I plan my work then I work my plan; then and then only does God's loving providence takes over. With my faith deepened by reading and hearing God's Word (Ro 10:17), I chose to share my inspiration and deepened faith with others by writing my book, THE WORD OF GOD: JESUS CHRIST.

In this book I attempted to express a simple understanding of the omnipotence and infinite love, mercy and justice of the Father, and His providential plan for us all. I expressed how the Father did not create, but begot His Son, and the Father and Son's love mutually begot the Holy Spirit, all three Persons, yet one God (Heb. 1:5 & 5:5). I expressed how the Father's Son's mission was to give eternal life to those of us who believe in Him by becoming the slain lamb (Rev 12:11). I expressed how the Holy Spirit's mission was and continues to be witness for the Father's Son, Jesus Christ, the Messiah; and how from the start, as in the Old Testament, He inspired the prophets to inspire the people about the Messiah (Rev 19:10-11). And how subsequent to Christ's death, Resurrection and Ascension, The Holy Spirit chose to come at Pentecost to give the Apostles and Disciples His gifts and fruits of His Spirit (1Co12:8-10 & Ga5:22) so that they could be more bold, confident and skilled in implementing His Mission by giving witness for Jesus Christ. All Scripture is inspired (2Ti3:16) by the Holy Spirit. In this sense, The Holy Spirit composes God's revealed Word in the Bible and designates the writers of the Pentateuch, the prophets, David and Solomon, the Evangelists, Peter, James and Paul to record His inspiration, with their witness, skills and tradition. Jesus Christ is the Word of God. "Heaven and earth will pass away, but my words will never pass away Mt24:35." All words in the Bible are either His historical words or words directly or indirectly pertaining to Himself. Jesus Christ is the Word of God (Jn1:1-5 and Rev19:13).

There are six references in Isaiah that God is a jealous God. He wants to be worshipped as God with regularity and frequency. In giving God our worship, Paul tells us not to be spectators, but to be participants (1.Cor.10:16). I have always believed that Mass is the most profound way to worship God, yet as a daily communicant for over 60 years I was not sure that I was really participating at Mass until I discovered the most deeply intense manner with which we Catholics can really participate at Mass by my Bible study. We all fall short (Ro3:23) and we are all sinners. The person who says he is not a sinner is a liar. Sin is a violation of God's law (1Jn3:4). How can we see God when only the pure of heart will see God (Mt5:8)? We believe The Lamb of God washes our Hearts clean (Rev12:11). We believe this continued cleansing of our hearts is required until the end of times. We believe the ordained priests have the authority from the Apostles to our current bishops (Mt18:18 & Mt16) to consecrate bread and wine to become The Body and Blood of Jesus Christ. "For My Flesh is real food and My Blood is real drink. Whoever eats my flesh and drinks my blood lives in me, and I live in him Jn6:55-57." Christ commanded His ordained priests to, "Do this in Memory of Me Lk22:19." Subsequent to this consecration at Mass, as contained in the Eucharistic prayers, the priest says, We (I, the ordained priest and you the laity) offer to you Father this bread, now the body of Christ and the wine now the blood of Christ, as an acceptable sacrifice. This sacrifice connects with His once and for all sacrifice (He7:27) and as a community sacrifice continues until the end of times, cleansing our human nature.

St. Peter tells us we are a royal priesthood (1Pt2:19). St. Paul tells us to offer ourselves as a living sacrifice (Rom12:1). The ordained priest offers sacrifice in our community Mass to The Father. We who are a part of the Royal Priesthood (1Pt2:9) and who have fulfilled our baptism by dedicating and consecrating ourselves to God (Jesus Christ) (LV11:44), offer ourselves as a living sacrifice to The Father. As with the community sacrifice at Mass, we connect our sacrifice of ourselves to Christ's Original Sacrifice at Calvary. As with the community sacrifice at Mass, Jesus Christ as God, (I saw Satan fall (Lk10:18)) transcends over 2000 years and reports to His Father. I have done as you have asked. I have emptied myself (Phil 2:7) and have completed my mission (Jn4:34. Rev12:11). And Father, these are the sacrifices that have been connected with my once and for all sacrifice. These are the community sacrifices and individual sacrifices that have been connected with Jesus Christ's original sacrifice and once and for all sacrifice. Jesus Christ as High Priest offers to His Father and our Father our sacrifices connected with His own once and for all sacrifice (He7:27). Were we there? Not physically. Yet we were there with our sacrifices and will continue to be there with our community and individual sacrifices. This is our beyond comprehension manner of worship. We have an eternity to thank God for this privilege of worship.

These are my personal experiences that deepened my faith through this participation form of worship as a result of my Bible studies. These experiences are contained in my book: THE WORD OF GOD: JESUS CHRIST.

Incidentally, my book was discussed in a personal interview with Al Kresta on Catholic Radio on August 16, 2004 at 5:00pm,and on February 24,2007at 3.30 pm with Michael Voris on the St. Michael's Media WDTK Station and received papal apostolic recognition .

Andrew Linzey wrote and published The Sayings of Jesus through Ecco Press (1991). The book contained an introduction and ten topics. He ably organized Christ's words into clear divine and human relationships and provided a good, simple method of knowing Jesus Christ. He said that many of Jesus Christ's words can be paralleled elsewhere, as is in the Old Testament. I question his inference that His (Christ's) words were not unique. Unfortunately, there are many theologians who now maintain that Jesus' words were not unique.

However, we should refer to the basic belief with Christians contained in the first chapter of John's Gospel, that "The Word created all things and that Word became flesh and dwelt among us. Before the world was created, the Word already existed; He was with God, and He was the same as God (John 1:1)." Christians believe that every word contained in Scripture is inspired (2 Timothy 3, 16). Though the words change as a result of different Bible translations, the words containing the message, are always inspired by the Holy Spirit. These references support the deep solid faith that the Son of God, who became man, is truly the Word contained in all Scripture. "I fell down at his feet to worship him, but he (the angel) said to me, 'don't do it! I am a fellow servant of yours and of your brothers, all those who hold to the truth that Jesus revealed. Worship God' for the truth that Jesus revealed is what inspired the prophets (Revelation 19:10)."

We Christians believe that this same Word was "begotten" by the Father and, with mutual love, proceeded to the Holy Spirit. We Trinitarian Christians believe that these are three real persons, yet one God. We Christians believe that the basic mission of the Holy Spirit is to give witness to and for the Son of God, Jesus Christ, the Word.

This belief has support from John 16:7, "Unless I go, the Holy Spirit will not come." Christ's message was that if the Holy Spirit came before He completed His mission, that is, having suffered, died, risen, and ascended, the Holy Spirit would give only partial witness for Him. Consequently, the Holy Spirit chose to come at Pentecost (50 days after Christ's resurrection) to inspire complete witness for Christ, the Word. The Spirit gave His gifts and fruits to Christ's apostles and followers to implement His mission of giving witness for Christ. This same Holy Spirit inspired all of the authors and writers of the Old Testament to prophesy and inspire His Chosen People about the Messiah, His nature, and His coming to cleanse His people (Is 53:6 & Ps 51:1&5). This supports our deep belief that the Messiah, the Word, the Son of God, Jesus Christ are all the same, directly and indirectly contained in all Scripture as the Word. This same Word became the historical Jesus Christ. Eye Witnesses were inspired by the Holy Spirit to record the words of Jesus in the New Testament. Though St. Paul was not an eyewitness to the activities of the historical Jesus, he was given special visions and inspirations to write his epistles about Jesus Christ and His words (1 Cor. 2:9).

CHAPTER I

The Father

The Father is the 'unoriginated' origin, the one who eternally has begotten His Son, the Son of God; proceeding from the eternal love of the Father for His Son and the Son's eternal love for His Father comes the eternal communion of their life and love, the Holy Spirit. We Trinitarian Christians believe that the Father, Son of God, and Holy Spirit are three individual persons, each of Whom contain and possess the entire essence of one God, each of Whom are in an eternal bond of love with the other two persons of God.

This only God is infinite, incomprehensible, eternal, and simple in his absolute essence, immense, illimitable, omnipresent and omnipotent. This one God contains all knowledge, beauty, understanding, sweetness, providence, justice, mercy, happiness, holiness and wisdom. His universe expresses His greatness and magnificence and wonders. God is love (1 John 4:16). We humans love because God first loved us (1 John 4:19). God gives us humans grace, enabling us to believe in His Son and be saved from our self-destruction, with no credit to ourselves (Eph 2:8). God's love is infinite, as are all His attributes. If we could put the love of everyone who ever lived, are living, and will live into the heart of our parents for us, God's love for us would still be infinitely more.

God's plan was that we should all share His infinite love and Happiness. Yet because of our first parents' original sin (violation of God's law – 1 John 3:4) and our resulting tendency to do likewise, our condition had to be repaired. So, at the Father's appointed time, He sent His Son to transform our sinful condition precisely by accepting every aspect of it but sin (Is 53:5, John 3:16 & 2Cor 5:21) in order that everyone who believes in Jesus Christ, the Son of God, may not die but have eternal life. In God's plan, He made us in His image, including free will (the right to choose). Proverbs (16:9) reminds us that we are required to plan our work and work our plan, yet God's providence ultimately disposes. In other words, God is pro-choice with consequences (Deut 30:15). "Choose life or death" – choose God's law or our own selfish interests, choose heaven or hell. "Those who do not believe in me have condemned themselves (Mark 16:16)."

Further references in the Bible to the Father are as follows:

Gen 1:26 Ex 3:6 Ps 33:6 Is 6:3 Ex 33:20 Ex 34:6

CHAPTER II

The Father's Plan

❝My thoughts," says the Lord, "Are not like yours, and my ways are different from yours. As high as the heavens are above the earth, so high are my ways and thoughts above yours (Isaiah 55:8-9)." Yet the first three chapters in Genesis can help us begin to have a little better insight about the Father's plan. Though we are not historians all of scripture is inspired by the Holy Spirit, and is given to those who are privileged to record it. And even though some of the messages contained in the Bible appear to be contrary (never contradictory) because it's all inspired (2 Tim: 3:16), those of us, who have received the gift of discernment (1 Cor.12: 10), can understand the basic message. The Lord made Adam and Eve in His image, with the right of choice and consequence of their choices. He gave them the privilege of walking with him in paradise and eating from the tree of life on condition that they complied with His will, "Not to eat from a certain tree." They disobeyed the Lord, they sinned (1 John 3.4) and they received the consequence of being thrown out of paradise with Adam having to work by the "sweat of his brow" and provide for his wife, and Eve no longer being just a companion for Adam but also being subject to him. Yet the Lord gave them hope as they left paradise, in the conclusion of Genesis 3. The Lord prophesied that the snake (Satan) would snap at the woman's heel, and the seed of the woman (the Messiah-Jesus Christ, The Father's Son) will crush the snake (Satan). The prophets continued to give his chosen people hope about the coming of the Messiah, and the requirement to recognize and keep the Lord ONE in their lives. In Genesis 15, the Lord gave Abram grace to believe in Him, and as a result of his faith in the Lord, the Lord called Abram "righteous." In Genesis 17, the Lord now called him Abraham and made a covenant with him. The Lord told Abraham He would be God for him and his descendants, and would bless His chosen people and their descendants (including us Christians Gal.3.29) and required His chosen people to be circumcised. This was their outward sign instituted by God to give them grace for their faith to believe that the Lord is their one and only God and that He is the only One they recognize and worship. In Genesis 22, the Lord requested Abraham to sacrifice his son Isaac, who was his most valuable relationship. Without hesitation, Abraham prepared and proceeded to sacrifice his son, when an angel of the Lord told him not to hurt the boy. He told Abraham the Lord was pleased that he was willing to sacrifice his most important relationship, his only son, to the Lord. The essence of Abraham's covenant with the Lord was he recognized that in exchange for the Lord's promise of countless blessings for him and his descendants, He was required to be willing to give the Lord his most valuable assets, including his only son. We are all required to use Abraham's example, and be willing to give and continue to give our most valuable assets to the Lord, in exchange for His unlimited love. In reality, He will take better care of our valuable assets than we can.

A good definition of God is contained in Exodus 34:6-7. God is all Merciful and all Just. An example of His justice was in Exodus 32:32 when Moses prayed in intercession for his people for having worshipped the golden calf. The Lord wants us to pray fully and intercede for one another (1 Tim.2: 1). The Lord consented not to exterminate the people with the understanding that He would not forget what they did, and would eventually punish them.

For the Jews, His chosen people, Jr 31:31-34, gives a profound, and somewhat contrary type prophecy. The Lord says, "The time is coming when I will make a new covenant with the people of Israel and with the people of Judah. It will not be like the old covenant that I made with their ancestors when I took them by the hand and led them out of Egypt. Although I was like a husband to them, they did not keep that covenant. The new covenant that I will make with the people of Israel will be this: I will put my law within them and write it on their Hearts. I will be their God, and they will be my people. None of them will have to teach his fellow countryman to know the Lord, because all will know me, from the least to the greatest. I will forgive their sins and I will no longer remember their wrongs. I, the Lord, have spoken." At one time the Lord chose not to forget his people's wrongs and eventually punish them, and at another time the Lord chose to forgive and forget his people's wrongs. How can this contrary be reconciled? The Prophecy of Isaiah 53:4-10 can do it. "But he endured the suffering that should have been ours, the pain that we should have borne. But because of our sins he was wounded, beaten because of the evil we did. We are healed by the punishment he suffered, made whole by the blows he received. All of us were like sheep that were lost, each of us going his own way. But the Lord made the punishment fall on Him, the punishment all of us deserved. He was treated harshly, but endured it humbly; he never said a word. Like a lamb about to be slaughtered, like a sheep about to be sheared, he never said a word." This person who reconciles the contrary contained in Exodus 32:32 and in Jr. 31:31-34, and the person who Isaiah refers to in his Isaiah 53:4-10 is none other than the Messiah, Jesus Christ, the Son of God. He was the person the Father requested to empty Himself (Phil 2:7) In the Father's justice, He required complete payment and compensation for all sins. So He requested His only Son to accomplish this complete cleansing. The Son of God, while retaining the nature of God, given to Him by His Father when He was begotten by the Father before time began, became a human person, with the Virgin Mary's consent (Luke 1), yet never sinned by violating God's will and law (2 Cor. 5:21). And those of us who love and believe in Christ and comply with his commandments (John 14:15) are washed in His blood (Rev. 7:14) and have salvation, no credit to ourselves (Eph. 2:8-9). However, those who do not believe in Jesus Christ have condemned themselves (Mark 16:16).

Suffering, experienced to some extent by all of us humans, results in some misunderstandings. We have heard it said why could a good loving God permit the misery resulting from wars and so called acts of God? Because we are made in His image (Genesis 1:27) we have choice with consequences. Humans have on occasion created their own living hell. As a result of original sin, God permits this and serious health conditions such as Down Syndrome, epilepsy, palsy and finally physical death. "For sin pays its wage-death (Romans 6:23)." Yet frequently our own physical complications are the result of our own addictions. One of the hardest requests in scripture to accomplish is to thank God for everything (Eph. 5:20). How do we thank God for suffering? First it is reality, secondly we get God into our suffering condition through prayer. The Lord wants us who believe to have hands laid on the sick for healing (Mark 16:18). Healing is a gift from the Holy Spirit (1 Cor. 12:9). The Lord wants us to ask for healing and expect results (Matt. 7:7). Our faith contained in our prayers can move mountains (Matt 21:21). The Lord may choose to suspend the laws of nature and give healing. If the sick person does not receive healing, with the Holy Spirit's gift of discernment (1 Cor. 12:8) the sick person can react in the Spirit positively, retaining his child-like trust in the Lord's love and providence, and become spiritually stronger. In any event the sick person should use every opportunity to offer him/her self as a living sacrifice (Romans 12:1) and connect his sacrifice to Christ's once and for all sacrifice (Heb. 7:27). Jesus Christ who is with us always in time (Matt. 28:20) receives this "living sacrifice" and Christ as God, having no past nor future, transcends over 2000 years, and He reports to His Father, "Father in your hands I place my Spirit (Luke 23:46)." As He completes His mission of cleansing us in His blood, our "living sacrifices" have been connected to His once and for all sacrifice at that moment. We have participated in this most profound contin-uous prayer (1 Cor. 10.16). We were there; we are there and will continue to be there, with, in, and through Christ for the Father. Christ's mission was unique. The Father requested His Son to suffer and die once for all of us. As the Father's children, He does not want us to suffer. What Father wants his children to suffer? The Father wants us to have only love, joy and peace, not suffering. Yet the last thing Christ requested for all of us in Matt 28:19-20 and Acts 1:7 GIVE WITNESS FOR ME. The Father wants each one of us to give witness for His Son. The Holy Spirit will lead us to do this as we should, and He will inspire us to speak and relate to others, as we should (Matt. 10:18). Giving witness for Christ may result in suffering as it did for His apostles and other martyrs. If we suffer while giving witness for Jesus Christ we comply with the Father's will. In doing this we participate with Christ (1 Cor. 10:16) in repairing the broken body of Christ. We continue this till the final prophecy is accomplished (1 Cor. 15:24). "Christ will overcome all spiritual rulers, authorities, and powers and will hand over the Kingdom to God the Father. For Christ must rule until God defeats all enemies and puts them under His feet." Before this final prophesy is completed there is pain, blood and suffering, while we Christians are privileged to participate with Christ in repairing the broken body of Christ. As with Paul we thank God and glory in our sufferings, (Col. 1:24) because we more completely unite with our leader, Jesus Christ. And as with Peter, we thank God and are happy for our sufferings while giving witness for Jesus Christ (1 Peter 3:14, 4:13-14). When this final prophecy is completed, we who have followed the Holy Spirit in giving witness for Jesus Christ will have an eternity of LOVE, JOY AND PEACE, with the Holy Trinity, and their angels and saints.

CHAPTER III

The Son of God

We Christians believe that Jesus Christ is, by nature, the only Son of God, that He was begotten – not made – by the Father (Heb 1.5), and that He is one in being with the Father. We believe that through Jesus Christ, all things were created (John 1:3 Col 1:16). By the power of the Holy Spirit, He was born of the Virgin Mary (Luke 1:35) and became man (John 1:14 2 Cor 5:21). As a result of the original sin and our continued sin, that is, the violation of God's law(1John3:4), the Father sent His Son to free us from sin and restore our communion with the Father by His sufferings (Is 53:6) and death on the cross: by His Pascal mystery, we are reconciled to the Father and become His sons and daughters by grace.

Since Jesus Christ is God, He is not confined by space and time as we are; He is eternal. In Genesis 3, our first parents chose to violate God's law, which resulted in the original sin which, in turn, has contributed to the tendency and pattern for us all to do things our way rather than God's: our tendency to violate God's law. The admirable David, courageous shepherd boy, composer of psalms, and great king, expressed in Psalm 51:5, "I was conceived and born in sin"; Psalm 51:1, "Lord, cleanse me from my sin." As with David, God has given all of us enough grace to recognize our need for cleansing, the desire to be cleansed by the cleanser, Jesus Christ (Romans 3:24). Isaiah prophesied (53:5), "I will send my suffering servant to cleanse you and make you whole." He prophesied the coming of the Messiah, the Son of God, Jesus Christ, and the Word made flesh. We believe that three days after His death, Christ rose again from the dead as He had predicted (Luke 18:33). Our belief is supported by 500 witnesses (Corinthians 15:6).

In fulfillment of the Scriptures, He ascended into heaven and returned to the life He always had with His Father and that He will come to judge the living and the dead, and His kingdom will have no end (Luke 24:50, Acts 1:9, Matt 25: 31-46).

Jesus Christ as the Son of God did empty Himself from His full manifestation of His divinity when He became a human life fetus in the womb of the Virgin Mary.(Phillip2:7&8) He still remained the Son of God. I saw Satin fall(Luke10:18)and before Abraham was I Am, and I Am Who Am(John 8:28&58).He acquired two natures. He remained the Son of God, having God's nature, and simultaneously acquired the additional human nature as Jesus Christ. As human, Jesus Christ became our friend(John15:15 as we try to become more of His friend. When we fulfilled our baptism He became our brother(Matt.28:10).He stands up for us and acknowledges us as we are required to do for Him.(Matt 10:32-33) He is our physician(Matt9:12).He knows what is wrong for us and wants to provide us with the right solution if we would open our heart for His grace to do so. He wants our burden(Matt.11:28)and we have the choice of keeping it for ourselves or giving it to Him. He is lover John4:7&14)With God's providence, we probably have experienced the real spark of His love.(1 John4:19)We have experienced real love from our parents, guardians or friends at one or more times in our lives. This enables us to know the difference between real love and phony love and compels us to want more of His Real Love. Jesus Christ is the one who cleanses our hearts enabling us to see and be with Himself and His Father, the Source of Love for eternity(Matt5:8). .

For other references to the Son, see:

Mt 9:6 Mk 8:31 Mt 1:1 Mt 1:21 Mt 3:17 Mk 1:1
Jn 1:1 Acts 20:25 Lk 4:18 Jn 5:7 Acts 9:5 John 1:34
Jn 8:28 Jn 8:58 Lk 10:18 Jn 14:6

CHAPTER IV

Sacred Heart of Jesus

On the first Friday subsequent to the Sunday recognizing the most holy body and blood of Christ known as Corpus Christi Sunday, the church recognizes the Sacred Heart of Jesus. How did this expression originate? In 1675 at the Visitation Convent in Paray-Le-Monial, France, Jesus Christ appeared to Sister Margaret Mary Alacoque. He asked her to make public the details of His love for all. With the help of Father Claude DeLaColumbiere, Margaret Mary's Jesuit confessor, she recorded the messages contained in the Apparitions, which were later approved by the church as reliable and authentic. During these apparitions, Jesus showed Margaret Mary His Heart pierced with thorns and on fire with love. He told her this image graphically demonstrates His unlimited, unconditional, and sacrificial love for all. He expressed His sadness that people have failed to read and accept the many scriptural references of His unlimited, unconditional, and sacrificial love for us all. He asked her to communicate His detailed love image to all. Moreover,

Jesus gave her twelve promises for those who accept and give witness for His love and Sacred Heart.

1) I will give them the necessary graces for their state in life.
2) I will give peace in their homes.
3) I will comfort them in their afflictions.
4) I will be their secure refuge in life and death.
5) I will give abundant blessings on all they do.
6) I give sinners my mercy without limit.
7) Tepid souls will grow fervent
8) Fervent souls will become more perfect.
9) I will bless every place where the image of my Heart is visibly honored
10) I will give priests the gift of touching the most hardened hearts.
11) Those who promote My Sacred Heart's love shall have their names written in my Heart, never to be blotted out.
12) I will give the grace of final penitence to those who receive Holy Communion on the first Friday of nine consecutive months.

St. Margaret Mary and St. Claude DeLaColumbiere were both canonized in the 20th century. Incidentally, these 12 promises were recorded in the 1974 Catholic Almanac, and are all contained in scripture directly or indirectly.

In John 1:12, "Those who accept and believe in the Word, are given the right to become the Father's sons and daughters, not because they are born of a natural father, but because they accept and believe in the Word, are they given this right." There is a difference between the right to vote and vote, and the right to eat and eat. So too there is a difference between the right and really exercising this right to become the Father's sons and daughters. Christ asked His Father to

"Dedicate them to the truth, Your Word is truth (John 17:17)." Jesus is the Word and the Truth. Peter requests us to "Consecrate ourselves to Christ (1.Peter 3:15)." When we commit to Christ we become the Father's sons and daughters.

Should any have interest in the, "Enthronement" of the Sacred Heart, that is consecrating and dedicating yourself and family to the Sacred Heart, please contact the local representative of the "Men of the Sacred Heart" at 248-642-1880.

CHAPTER V

The Holy Spirit

The Holy Spirit is the third person of the Holy Trinity. The Father and the Son's love for one another mutually begot the Holy Spirit. And so, the Holy Spirit has the same nature as the Father and the Son of God, and becomes the third person in One God as contained in this Holy Trinity. The Holy Spirit gives witness to and reveals the Father and His Son, Jesus Christ. In Genesis, 1:2, we see the Holy Spirit playing a role in the drama of creation. The Holy Spirit inspired the prophets to instruct the people regarding God, His law, and the coming of the Messiah, Jesus Christ(Rev.19;10). The Holy Spirit inspired all of the writers of the Old Testament to record God's message of justice, love and mercy. The Holy Spirit overshadowed Mary when the Angel Gabriel told her that the Father wanted her to be the Mother of His Son. When Mary questioned how this could be, the Angel explained that the Holy Spirit would come upon her and thus her child would truly be the Son of God. The Holy Spirit helped John the Baptist identify Jesus as the Messiah, the Son of God, "You will see the spirit come down in the symbol of a dove and stay on a man; He is the one who baptizes with the Holy Spirit." "I have seen it," said John. "And I tell you that He is the Son of God (John 1:33-34)."

The Holy Spirit led Jesus Christ out into the desert to fast and pray and be tempted by the devil for 40 days (Luke 4:1-2) The Holy Spirit confirmed Jesus Christ's baptism when he descended as a dove.

At the same moment, the Father also manifested His blessing as He spoke from Heaven (Luke 3:21-22).

A very significant reference to the Holy Spirit are the words of Jesus, "Unless I go, the Holy Spirit will not come (John 16:7)." These words show that one of the Holy Spirit's primary missions is giving witness to and revealing Jesus Christ as the Son of God. As promised, the Holy Spirit descended on Pentecost, that is, 50 days after the resurrection and the ascension. He came to give the apostles the gifts and fruits of His Spirit, enabling them to give vigorous and bold witness to the risen Christ.

A fuller discussion of the gifts of the Holy Spirit can be found in 1 Corinthians 12:8-10; wisdom, understanding, faith, knowledge, discernment, healing and tongues. The fruits of the Holy Spirit are referred to in Galatians 5:22 – love, joy, peace, patience, kindness, goodness, truthfulness, justice, character and faithfulness. Neither money nor education can acquire these gifts and fruits. These are solely the gifts and fruits of the Holy Spirit for those who believe in Jesus Christ, the Word of God, and have consecrated (1 Pt 3:15) and dedicated (John 17:17) themselves to Him. And, in that manner, they have become new creations (2 Cor 5:17).

We give evidence we are born again and have become a new creation when we are impelled to give witness for Jesus Christ. 2 Cor5:14

The Holy Spirit is also mentioned in:

1 Cor 2:10 Jn 15:25 Gn 1:2 Rom 5:5 Phil 3:3
Acts 13: 2-3 Jn 14:16f Lk 1:35 Lk 3:22 Lk 4:1
Jn 1:32-33 Jn 16:7 Jn 16:13 Acts 2:3-4 1Cor 12:4f
Gal 5:22 Jn 3:5 Acts 2:17 Joel 2:28-32

CHAPTER VI

Mary

Mary, the mother of Jesus Christ, is perhaps, the most misunderstood person in the Bible. Some bristle at her very name because they fear a violation of the First Commandment (i.e., her being excessively honored, as much as God). Others appear to worship her, that is, reverence her and pray to her to the exclusion of her Son, Jesus. Both of these are adverse and extreme perceptions of Mary. Let's reflect on the clear messages contained in Scripture, a message that is very balanced.

The Angel Gabriel informed Mary that the Father wanted her to be the mother of His Son, a man who would be called Jesus. Mary asked how this mission was to be accomplished. The Angel replied that she would conceive through the Holy Spirit. Mary agreed to the Lord's will (Luke 1:26-36). Some question Mary's title as ever – Virgin Mary. The virginity of Mary before the Incarnation is an essential dogma of our faith; otherwise, Jesus would be Her child, not the only Son of the eternal Father. Critics of Mary's virginity quote Mark (3:31-33), "...and they said to

Him, your mother and your brothers and sisters are outside, and they want you." It is basic understanding that in the Middle Eastern culture, relatives and sometimes even close neighbors are considered brothers and sisters. The point of Mary as "ever – Virgin," that is Virgin even after Christ's birth is standard Catholic teaching.

As Mary is the mother of the Son of God, Jesus, it is basically understandable that she has maternal influence over her Son. John (2:1-10) records the wedding feast in Cana, where Mary observed that the hosts had run out of wine. Jesus replied, "Woman, how does this concern of yours affect me? My time has not yet come (John 2:4)." Undeterred by Jesus' reply, Mary told the servants, "Do whatever he tells you (John 2:5)." Jesus said to the servants, "Fill these jars with water (John 2:7)." When the man in charge of the feast tasted the water now changed into wine, he told the bridegroom, "You have kept the best wine 'til now (John 2:10)." Ask children why Jesus would change water into wine when he had clearly told His mother that His time had not yet come to do the miracles. Eight out of ten will give you the correct answer; He did the miracle to please His mother.

In Mary's frequent apparitions over the centuries, she has always encouraged praying the Rosary. The full Rosary includes 15 "Our Fathers" (Mt 6:5) and 15 groupings of 10 "Hail Mary's" which refer to various experiences in the lives of Mary and Jesus; the usual accepted format for the Rosary is one third of the entire 15 decades. Recently, John Paul suggested another five decades focused on Christ's ministry. Where in Scripture do we find the Hail Mary? The first part is contained in Luke (1:25-36), while the second part is in Paul's first letter to (1 Timothy 2:1). "Make intercessory prayer for all," Paul said. Mary is another Christian – the help of Christians – so she does what we are requested to do: make intercessory prayers for all so that all can be saved (1 Timothy 2:4). However, as we see referred in John (2:1-10),

Mary, His mother, has more influence with her Son than we do in our intercessory prayers.

In Romans 8:14, Paul asks us all to be led by the Holy Spirit to give evidence that we are the Father's sons and daughters by grace. What better way to do this than have Mary, as spouse of the Holy Spirit, assist us with her intercessory prayers. I have personally experienced the suspension of the laws of nature with Mary's intercessory prayers for my intentions. Furthermore, as all mothers help condition their children physically, materially and spiritually, so does our mother Mary help us. Mary was conceived without original sin and therefore completely open to the Holy Spirit. We too, can invoke the Holy Spirit, although to a lesser degree than Mary, by being pure, i.e., having a single priority a pure intention. For additional information on Mary, see the Bible at:

Gn 3:15 Ps 45:10 Sir 24 Is 7:14 Jn 2:1-10
Lk 1:46-56 Mt 1:16 Rev 12

CHAPTER VII

The Assumption of the Blessed Virgin Mary

In Matt. 21:21 Jesus Christ tells us with faith we can move mountains. In Romans 10:17 we read that by reading and hearing God's word we develop more faith in Jesus Christ. Yet Catholics were given as a defined article of Faith on November 1, 1950, that Mary's glorified body and soul, subsequent to her death or some kind of rest, was taken up into Heaven. Catholics refer to this as the Assumption of the Blessed Virgin Mary. Even to this day, her Assumption has been supported by the commonly accepted early church tradition.

The first Church of the Assumption, a countryside chapel in the Kidron Valley was built some time about the beginning of the fifth century and consecrated by the Patriarch of Jerusalem, Juvenal (422-458) just after the Council of Calcedon (431). Thereafter a new Church was built over the tomb of Mary which became the crypt in which was venerated the Tomb of the Virgin. The upper church was completely destroyed before the arrival of the Crusaders. When the

Crusaders arrived they found only a small edifice. Godfrey deBouillon built a monastery here, the well-known abbey of St. Mary of the Valley of Jehoshaphat for the Benedictines of Cluny, to whose care he entrusted the Church. The Crusaders rebuilt the Church about the year 1130. This Church of the Tomb of the Virgin was again destroyed together with the monastery by Saladin after 1187.

The ruin of the sacred monument would nonetheless have been inevitable, mainly because of the floods that continuously damaged it, had not the Franciscans entered into the possession of the Church in the second half of the fourteenth century. Until the seventeenth century the Franciscans maintained the Tomb of the Virgin. Since 1757 the Greek Orthodox rite have enjoyed the possession of the venerable shrine, which they shared with the Armenians. During the years 1907–1909 Farther Prosper Viaud, O.F.M. directed further excavations. He discovered mosaics and graffiti of many devout pilgrims and Crusader capitals, which today are preserved in the adjacent museum.

In 1955 the late Fr. Bellarmino Bagatti, O.F.M., professor at the Studium Biblicum Franciscanum at Flagellation, Jerusalem, began exhaustive archaeological examination of the whole area prior to the erection of the new basilica of the Church of the Assumption. Operations continued until 1968 and confirmed the history of The Tomb of The Virgin Mary, and became the most documented of all sanctuaries of the Holy Land.

Regarding the time and manner of Our Lady's death, nothing certain is known. The earliest known literary reference to the Assumption is found in the Greek work "DeObitu S. Dominae." This is an apocryphal treatise from the fourth or fifth century containing the name of St. John. This is referred to in the sermons of St. Andrew of Crete, St. John Damascene, St. Modestus and St. Gregory of Tours.

Please reference www.newadvent.org and www.chris-trex.org and the Catholic Encyclopedia for more support and further information on this topic.

.

Chapter VIII

Humanity

We humans receive the essence of our nature from our parents, and they from their parents, "et cetera" all the way back to our first parents. We are not historians, yet we Christians believe in God's creation as expressed in the Bible. We believe God originally created the first two humans biblically known as Adam and Eve (Genesis 1:26). God gave Adam and Eve residence in the Garden of Eden with a condition that they were not permitted to eat of the tree that gives knowledge of what is good and evil (Genesis 2:17). We do not know the historical details, yet we do know that in some way Adam and Eve violated God's requirements (Genesis 3:6). Disobeying God's law is sin (1 John 3:4). Adam and Eve sinned.

Paul tells us in Romans 6:23, the wages of sin is death. From that time on Adam and Eve and their descendents are physically destined to die. As with our parents we are all under the influence of Adam and Eve's original sin. We are all physically born to die. Even the great David, the courageous volunteer who stood up to Goliath, the mighty and fearsome Philistine warrior, the great King, the inspired David who wrote the Psalms, this same David recognized he was under the influence of original sin. He expresses in his Psalm 51:5-6, "I was conceived and born in sin;" and in the first verse of that same Psalm, he says, "Lord, cleanse me." If David needed cleansing, we all do . . . How are we purified? Isaiah (53:5-6) tells us, "I will send my suffering servant to cleanse you and make you whole." Who is this, the One whom the Father sent to make us whole? He is Jesus Christ, the Son of God, and every word in Scripture directly or indirectly refers to Him.

God did give Adam and Eve (and their descendents) hope as they were removed from paradise when He gave the first biblical prophecy in Genesis 3:15. The woman and her offspring will be in combat against the snake understood as Satan. The snake will bite her heel, yet her offspring (Jesus) will crush the snake. The prophets in the Old Testament predicted the Messiah, and Jesus Christ fulfilled their prophecy. This was the Father's plan that has always given hope. When we complete our baptism by dedicating ourselves to Jesus Christ (John 17:17 and 1 Peter 3:15) we become new creations (2. Cor. 5:17) by being born of water and the Spirit (John 3:5). We then acquire our second nature, which becomes born to live. In Romans 7:14-25, Paul graphically shows his human nature by ascribing his frustration in that he does the things he does not want to do and does not do the things he wants to do. Yet he experiences freedom from the "Law of sin and death" through the "Law of the Spirit, which brings us life in union with Christ Jesus (Romans 8:2 and 2 Cor 3:6 & Jn 1:12 & 13)." So with our sinful human nature (John 1:12-13) when we believe in Jesus Christ, and dedicate and consecrate ourselves to His Father's Word, which is Jesus Christ, (John 17:17), we fulfill and complete our baptism and are born to live as new creations (2 Cor. 5:17).

CHAPTER IX

Baptism

As the Lord chose to separate His "chosen people" by requiring eight-day-old infant boys and "Every male among you" (including slaves) to be circumcised, so, too, the Lord wanted to separate His followers from immoral people, including those who say they believe in Jesus Christ yet visibly violate God's law (1 Cor. 5:9, 1 Jn 3:4). The beginning of this separation process began when the Word of the Lord came to John the Baptist to call people to a baptism of repentance (Lk 3:2) and fulfill the prophesy of (Isaiah 40:3-5) by preparing the way of the Lord. Some references record that "All Jerusalem" confessed their sins and were baptized by John (Mt 3:5 Mk 1:5). Jesus Himself gave the example of being baptized by John (Lk 3:21). The Father and the Holy Spirit witnessed in support of this event (Lk 3:22).

When Paul was at Philippi preaching the Gospel, he was jailed for disturbing the Jews. While continuing his ministry in jail, he so impressed the jailer that this individual asked the most important question in Scripture: "What must I do to be saved?" Paul told him to believe in the Lord Jesus Christ

(Acts 16:30-31). After a brief instruction, the jailer became so intent that; "He had Paul baptize him and his family that very hour at night (Acts 16:33)." Incidentally, this passage gives us authority to baptize infants: the jailer, as husband and father, had the authority to have his wife and children baptized. With that authority came responsibility of giving formation to his wife and children to help them live out their baptism by helping them know, love and commit themselves to Jesus Christ as the most important person in their lives who brings them to the Father (John 14:6). This is required because only by accepting and believing and committing to the Word, Jesus Christ, can we become sons and daughters of the Father (John 1:12). In his priestly prayer at the Last Supper Jesus prayed, "Father, dedicate my followers in the truth. Father, Your word is truth (John 17:17)." He was asking His Father to give grace to His followers to dedicate themselves to Himself, Who is the way, the truth and the life because no one comes to the Father except through the Son (John 14:6). In his first Epistle Peter (3:15) also requests that we consecrate ourselves to Jesus Christ. In John (3:5), Christ adds an important requirement to John's baptism of water – "Unless you are baptized with water and the spirit, you cannot enter the kingdom of heaven." How is this accomplished? Throughout the Bible, the Holy Spirit gives witness to the Word, i.e., the Son of God, Jesus Christ, the Messiah. In John 16:7, Jesus said, "Unless I go, the Holy Spirit will not come." This appears to be a contrary comment because the Holy Spirit had already come, giving preliminary witness to the Word and coming upon the Virgin Mary so that the Word might become flesh. But Christ's message was that He had to suffer, die and rise again three days after His crucifixion – He had to complete His mission before the Holy Spirit would come and give complete witness for Him.

This event occurred at Pentecost (50 days after His resurrection from the dead). The Holy Spirit chose to come this time to give Christ's followers the gifts (1 Cor 12:8-11) and fruits (Gal. 5:22) so that they could more powerfully implement His mission by giving witness for Jesus Christ. When they received these gifts and fruits of the Spirit, they became a new creation (2 Cor. 5:17), being "Born Again" in the Spirit. We, too, become "Born Again" in the Spirit when we dedicate and consecrate ourselves to Jesus Christ, and to the Holy Spirit. Doing so, we fulfill our baptism and become holy(lev.40:31)(holy is a synonym for the word integrity). The Spirit gives us a new creation and as a result we are born to live. The Spirit strengthens our commitment to Christ with His Gifts and fruits and supports us in giving more effective witness for Jesus Christ.

"Sacramental Seeds" can be better understood by the parable of the sower, in Mark's fourth chapter. Some of his seeds fell on the road and the birds ate them (i.e. Satan takes them). Some of the seeds fell on rocky ground (i.e. the seed was received impetuously and given up). Some seeds fell in the bush, which choked the growth of the seed (i.e. the cares of the world became the important concern). Some seeds fell on good ground, and the seeds flourished and multiplied (i.e. God's word is received and the multiplication of fruit results).

In this parable the seed, wherever it is sown, contains the same good quality. The seed becomes effective only in good soil. How can our soul become as good soil? How can it receive God's word and have it become deeply rooted? With God's grace, and we all have more than enough grace, (2 Corinthians 9:8), we can and should commit to Jesus Christ as the most important person in our lives. Why is He our most important person? Whether we acknowledge it or not, we all need and want more life and love, and the source of this is the Father. Jesus Christ asks us, "Do we want to go to the Father?" He says, "I am the way, the truth, and the life, no one goes to the Father except through Me (John 14:6)."

Jesus Christ is our only key to complete life and love. So our Christian first commandment is to put Jesus Christ as number one in our lives. "Whatever you do, do it for the Lord Jesus Christ (Col. 3:17 & 23, 1 Cor. 10:31)." When we commit to Jesus Christ as the most important person in our lives, we complete our baptism and "accelerate" our confirmation and rebirth in the Holy Spirit.

What is the connection between our pure intention and our rebirth in the Spirit? Subsequent to Pentecost, the Holy Spirit's mission is to give witness for Jesus Christ. When the Spirit sees our commitment to Jesus Christ, He gives us His gifts and fruits which money cannot buy, nor education acquire, so that we can better implement His mission. As a result we are born again.

Baptism is also mentioned in the Bible at:

Mt 28:19 Rom 6:3-6 Eph 5:26 Col 2:12-14 Eph 4:5
Acts 2:38 Heb 10:22 Jn 3:5 Mk 1:4-9 Mt 3:11 Mt 3:14-15

CHAPTER X

Sons and Daughters of God

C aiaphas, the Jewish high priest, asked Jesus, "Are you
the Son of God?" Jesus answered, "I am. And you will
see the Son of Man seated at the right hand of the Almighty and
coming in the clouds of heaven (Mk 14:61-62)." Jesus knew
His answer would condemn Him, yet because He is the way,
the truth and the life, it was the only answer He could give.
Caiaphas and the chief Jewish priests proceeded to condemn
Him, because they felt He was guilty of blasphemy.

In John (1:12), "Those who accept and believe in the
Word (the Son of God incarnate, Jesus Christ) are given
the right to become God's children, His sons and daughters, not because they were born of a natural father, but
because they accept and believe in the Word." It is one
thing to have the right to choose; yet it is more important
to exercise the right.

So too, it is one thing to have the right to become the sons
and daughters of God and quite another to actually become
sons and daughters of God. How can this actually be done?
In John (17:17), Christ asked His Father to dedicate His

followers in the truth. In the same request, He said, "Father, Your Word is truth." Christ's intent was that His Father would give grace to His followers to enable them to dedicate themselves to Him, the Way, the Truth and the Life (John 14:6) Peter, in his first epistle (3:15) asked us to consecrate ourselves to Jesus Christ. Christ said that if we love him, we will keep His commandments (John 14:15). So, to complete our baptism and realize our right to become the Father's sons and daughters by grace, we dedicate and consecrate ourselves to Jesus and to keeping His commandments.

There are some who are occasionally called "new agers," who believe they are sons and daughters of God by nature because they were created in His image and likeness (Gen 1:26). Because of their perception of being God's children by nature, they believe there was no original sin contrary to what David wrote in the Psalms, "Lord, I was conceived and born in sin (Psalm 51:5)." Due to the tendency to sin, that is violate God's law, (1 John 3:4) these confused people remain in the serious condition for the need of cleansing. Furthermore, these misguided people believe for themselves there is no consequence resulting from the breaking of God's law. They do not believe in God's final judgment that can send one to hell for eternity. Jesus Christ tells us in Luke 12:4, "I tell you my friends, do not be afraid of those who kill the body, but cannot afterward do anything worse. I tell you fear God who has the authority to put one into hell."

God's love for His children is also mentioned in the Scriptures at:

1 Jn 3:1-2 Wis 11:26 Hos 11:3-4 Mt 23:37 Lk 1:50
Jas 2:13 John 1 12-13 John 3:16 1 John 4:19

CHAPTER XI

The Papacy

S ome writers question whether Jesus actually intended
to found an organized church. They suggest instead that
He wanted to form a community of believers who would
share His own way of costly sacrifice and who would deny
themselves and take up their cross and follow Him (Mk 8:34
& 35) Yet, Jesus <u>did</u> intend to do more. He asked His apostles, "Who do you say I am?" Simon Peter answered, "You
are the Messiah, the Son of the living God." To this, Jesus
replied, "Blessed are you, Simon, son of Jonah, it is not flesh
and blood, but my Father in Heaven Who has revealed this to
you. And so I tell you that you are Peter (rock) and upon this
rock foundation I will build My Church, and not even death
or the gates of hell shall prevail against it. I will give you
the keys of the kingdom of heaven: what you bind on earth
will be bound in heaven, and what you loose on earth will be
loosed in heaven (Mt. 16:15-19)." With this authority, Jesus
Christ established the "papacy," which became known as the
Catholic Church, that is, the universal Church. We begin to
understand how this formation came about by reading the

Acts of the Apostles and the history of the first three centuries of the Church.The Pope is the head of the Catholic Church.God's word as expressed in sacred scripture gives authority for all activities contained in the Catholic Church which include all the sacraments,the Mass,(our community sacrifice,)Marian devotions including the rosary and the Pope's infallibility with matters of faith and morals.

Though there have been troubled times for the Catholic Church over 2000 years,the Pope has always been right in matters of faith and morals.And in our day he has been a beacon of truth for all, including the Communists and Islams.

The capacity of the Pope is touched upon in the Scriptures in the following places:

Lk 22:31 Mt 10:2 Acts 5:29 Jn 21:15-10 Mt 6:18-19

CHAPTER XII

Followers of Jesus Christ

I n John (6:29), "My Father requests one thing for you to
do: believe in Me, the One He has sent." This results in
the progression of accepting and believing in the Word (John
1:12), the essential condition of being baptized by water and
the Spirit (John 3:5), the dedication (John 17:17), the consecration of the believer to Jesus Christ (1 Peter 3: 15), receipt
of the gifts (1 Cor. 12:8-10) and fruits (Gal 5:22) of the Holy
Spirit, becoming the new creation in Christ (2 Cor. 5:17),
and being compelled to do good works (Cor. 5: 14, Jas 2:17)
– all as a result of God's grace with no credit to the believer
(Eph 2:8-9).

St. Peter well describes the beginner Christian in 1 Peter
2:2 "Be like newborn babies always thirsty for pure spiritual milk, so that by drinking it you may grow up and be
saved. One, who has achieved the constant thirst for God's
word, is like the newborn Christian. The person has already
achieved his new creation (2 Cor. 5:17) with his commitment
putting Jesus Christ One in his life, thereby completing his
baptism. At this level, the Holy Spirit comes to the person

and he begins to receive gifts (1 Cor 12:8-11) and fruits (Gal. 5:22) of the Holy Spirit. Yet, this level, good as it is, is only intended as the beginning.

God wants us to become His adult sons and daughters. We give evidence of this spiritual maturity by being, "Led by the Holy Spirit (Romans 8:14)." Jesus Christ is Head of our church, yet He did return to the Father, and clearly indicated that unless He did return to the Father, the Holy Spirit would not come (John 16.7) Why? The Holy Spirit had already come. The Holy Spirit did come at these events, the second verse in Genesis 1., the inspiration for the prophets and Old Testament heroes, Mary's receipt of the Holy Spirit for Christ's conception as the Son of Man, and the Holy Spirit's witnessing Christ's baptism, and leading Christ into the desert to fast and be tempted (Luke 4). Jesus Christ had to complete His mission before the Holy Spirit would come at Pentecost and give His precious gifts and fruits to enable us to give better witness for Jesus Christ, and thereby implement the Holy Spirit's mission. So the Spirit is now Lord in our militant earth church. We must all accept the Holy Spirit as Lord in our lives (2 Cor. 3:17) because the Holy Spirit wants to teach us all things (John 16:13) so that we truly can become better witnesses for Jesus Christ (Acts 1:7). Being led by the Holy Spirit is our real grace and blessing that enables us to fully participate in the beatitudes Christ referred to in Matt. 5. & Luke 6.

Jesus Christ graphically describes the importance of being united to Him in John 15:1-10. It contains the words, "I am the vine and you are the branch. If you are connected to Me, you will live and bear much fruit. If you are not connected to Me, you are dead." You will continue to exist through out eternity, but will continue to remain dead, as the branch separated from the tree remains dead. If the branch is separated from the tree, it must be grafted back onto the tree to live. So also if we are ever disconnected from Jesus

Christ we must be reconnected to Christ by our confession and repentance of sin and reformation of our faith in Jesus Christ and our resolution to improve our conduct. In our adoration of the Blessed Sacrament prayer time, let us reflect on this.

The followers of Jesus must also be connected to the Holy Spirit. This is accomplished by completing baptism with dedication and consecration to Jesus Christ (John 17:17 and 1 Peter 3:15). With this relationship to Jesus Christ achieved by grace, the Holy Spirit connects with this dedicated follower of Christ and relates to him as an implement and aide for His own mission: giving witness for, "The Word" Jesus Christ. And to assist this "New Creation (2 Cor. 5:17)," now born of water and the Spirit (John 3:5) to give more bold, confident and skilled witness for Christ, the Spirit gives what neither money nor education can buy, the gifts (1 Cor. 12:8-10) and fruits of the Spirit (Gal. 5:22).

Once connected to the Holy Spirit, how can that close relationship remain? After experiencing a new creation (2 Cor. 5:17) with our dedication to Christ in our Baptism, should we have the attitude, "I am saved," because I believe in Jesus Christ (John 3:16) without doing any "Spiritual exercises (1 Tim. 4:8)?" Would it be presumptuous to think we do not need to pray (Luke 21:36) "Pray always," nor read and hear God's word (Rom. 10:17), "Faith comes from hearing," nor fast (Mark 2:20), "You will fast," nor have fellowship with believers (1 John 1:3 and Math. 18:20) "Where two or more are gathered in my name, I am there with them," nor tithe (Malachi 3:10), "Bring the full amount of your tithes to the Temple," nor do good works (James 2:17), "If it (faith) is alone and includes no actions, then it is dead." It certainly appears it would be presumptuous to think we can stay connected to the Holy Spirit without doing these spiritual exercises.

Moreover, the connection with the Holy Spirit is certainly retained by receiving Jesus Christ's very own body in Holy Communion. Luke 22:19, "Do this in memory of Me," and John 6:55, "for my flesh is real food and My blood is real drink. Whoever eats My flesh and drinks my blood has eternal life." This is not done symbolically. The Priest has the authority (Matt. 18:18) to request the Holy Spirit to make this change from bread to the body of Jesus Christ. Holy Communion becomes the real body of Jesus Christ under the appearance of bread. Baptized Christians should only receive this Blessed Sacrament if they have no serious sins, yet when they confess, repent, reform and forgive others, the Lord does forgive them. Also they should not receive Holy Communion unless they really believe they are receiving the body of Jesus Christ. St. Paul cautions us in 1 Cor. 11:27, "It follows that if anyone eats the Lord's bread or drinks from His cup in a way that dishonors Him, he is guilty of sin against the Lord's body and blood."

Another reference to our being Christ's followers is from Mt 16:24, "If anyone wants to come with me, he must forget himself, carry his cross, and follow me."

The Reformation has separated the Protestants from the Catholics. Yet there has been a trend among Bible studies to study Jesus Christ:THE WORD OF GOD,and begin to become more united in our faith.(John 17:21)Catholics, from the Council of NICEA 325 AD,have accepted the Greek version with understanding that Tobit Judith Esther Wisdom of Solomon Sirach Baruch Macabees 1&2and Esdras 1&2are all inspired words of God.The Protestants have accepted the Hebrew version of Scripture which consider these works as Apocrypha.Yet we Catholics and Protestants do love Jesus Christ as expressed in His Word. Nevertheless ,we Catholics have a different form of worship.We have the Mass which is the most profound form of worship.Refer to the Chapter on Worship.

Other references to our being Christ's followers are to be found in:

Lk 9:3-5 Mk 9:35 Mk 8:34-35 John 20:21 Mt 28:18-20
Mt 9:37-38 Lk 10:19 Mk 2:19-20 Mt 24:23-24
Mt 23:1-12 Mk 3:13-19 John 17:6-26 Mt 11:28-30
John 14:15 John 14:5 John 14:14

CHAPTER XIII

Prayer

Aristotle, in his second book, Volume VIII, in his writing on the Soul, refers to contemplation as the most important activity that any human person can achieve. Mortimer J. Adler in his ninth (Great Books) guide book (third reading, second part) of his Great Ideas Program published by the Encyclopedia Britannica, Inc., supports this same concept of contemplation. Aristotle in his work NICOMACHEAN ETHICS, describes contemplation as the most effective way to achieve happiness.

Thomas A. Kempis, author of <u>The Following of Christ</u>, otherwise known as <u>The Imitation of Christ</u>, said he would rather feel compunction contained in contemplation rather than be able to define it. Yet in <u>The Collected Works of St. John of the Cross</u>, translated by Kieran Kavanaugh, O.C.D. and Otilio Rodriguez, O.C.D., published by the Institute of Carmelite Studies, Washington D.C., 1991, St. John of the Cross gives deep and comprehensive methods for contemplation, so that not only the contemplative, but also the lay person may understand and more thoroughly participate in the values of contemplation.

The theme of John of the Cross is contained in three progressive stages beginning with the purgative. In Mt 16:24, Jesus Christ gave us the first requirement should we choose to follow Him. We must deny ourselves. We must eliminate our selfish desires. With these achievements, we proceed into the second stage of illumination. With an open heart, within which one has denied one's selfish desires, and has opened oneself to God's grace to follow Jesus Christ, The Word, The Holy Spirit perceives in that person an implement for the Holy Spirit to give witness for Jesus Christ, which is basically the Holy Spirit's mission. So The Holy Spirit chooses to give that person His additional gifts and fruits (1Cor 12:8-11 & Gal. 5:22) to enable the person to become more skilled, bold and effective in giving witness for Jesus Christ. With this full illumination from the Holy Spirit this person experiences a beyond comprehension unity with Jesus Christ Himself. In this way this person experiences what St. Peter recorded in 2 Peter 1:3. He experiences a direct participation in the divinity of God Himself. With this beyond comprehension participation in Jesus Christ's divinity, this person has reached the ultimate level of prayer and contemplation.

The Apostles asked Jesus how to pray in Matthew (6:5-13) and Luke (11:2-4). Christ answered that they should not use a lot of words in long prayers, that "Your Father already knows what you need before you ask Him."

"When you pray, do not be like the hypocrites. They love to stand up and pray in the houses of worship and on the street corners, so that everyone will see them. I assure you, they have already been paid in full. But when you pray, go to your room, close the door, and pray to your Father, who is unseen. Your Father, who sees what you do in private, will reward you. When you pray, do not use a lot of meaningless words, as the pagans do, who think that God will hear them because their prayers are long. Do not be like them. Your Father already knows what you need before you ask Him" (Matt 6:5-9). In Matt 6:9 Jesus Christ teaches us His prayer: THE OUR FATHER. An additional advantage in going to our room for prayer is that we can eliminate distractions and can more effectively put ourselves in The Lord's presence. He proceeded to give them the "Our Father Prayer." There are different types of prayer: petition, thanksgiving, adoration, repentance, and intercession. A simple method is reading Scripture and reflecting (meditating) on God's message in a given passage. A similar method is the selection of important themes in the Life of Jesus as we do when praying the rosary, and meditating on these with the intention of arriving at some good aspirations and resolutions. The ultimate prayer is, "Praying as we should" (Rom 8:26). "The Holy Spirit comes to help us weak as we are. For we do not know how we ought to pray. The Holy Spirit Himself pleads with God for us in groans that words cannot express. And God, who sees our hearts, knows what the thought of the Spirit is because the Spirit pleads with God on behalf of his people and in accordance with His Will."

In other words, as we open ourselves to the Holy Spirit in prayerful contemplation, the Holy Spirit will give us deep insights, holy thoughts and appropriate resolutions. When we make requests in prayer, we should expect results (Mt 7:7 & 8). This takes solid faith in Christ. "Anything you ask for in My name, I will do it (Jn 14:14)." This kind of faith moves mountains (Mt 21:21). An important part of prayer is persistence. In Luke (18:1-8), the Lord Jesus gives us the Parable of the Widow and the Judge who does not believe in God; he could not care less about the widow. But because of her persistence, the judge gives her what she wants so he can get rid of her. "Now, will not God judge in favor of His own people who cry to Him day and night for help? Will He be slow to help them? I tell you, He will judge in their favor and do it quickly (Lk 18:1-7)."

Other references to prayer in the Scriptures include:

Jn 4:23-24 Mt 26:41 Lk 10:41-42 Mt 21:21-22
Lk 21:36 Gn 18:27 Jn 17:6-20 Mk 13:18-19
Rom 8:26 Mt 6:5-15 Mk 11:23 Mt 7:7-13 Mt 7:21

CHAPTER XIV

Worship

Loving the Lord with one's whole heart, soul, mind, and strength (Dt 6:5) has been and continues to be the foundation of the Jewish law and worship. This is emphasized more than once in Deuteronomy (30:15) and Joshua (24) in encouraging the chosen people to choose life rather than death, good rather than evil, and to serve, honor, and worship the one true God rather than His rival (pagan) gods. Over six times in Isaiah, God is described as a jealous God, One that does not tolerate a second-rate position. The First Commandment of putting God first in our lives is really given for our own benefit. We always self-destruct eventually if we violate the First Commandment.

The focal point of worship in the Old Law was the Ark of the Covenant. Only the Levites had the authority to handle and be custodians of the Ark. Not even the great King David could touch the Ark; and when, on the way from Hebron to Jerusalem, one of his soldiers attempted to stop the Ark from falling, this individual died upon touching it. (2 Samuel 6:6-7) Obviously, if everyone could touch the Ark, its worship would lose reverence; this would result in a reduction of the prayerful faith of the people. In Hebrews 7, the author describes what a priest was and is from Melchizedek through the Levites to Jesus Christ. Basically, a priest is one who represents his people (his family, friends, those whom he has been asked to pray for) before God; on behalf of his community, he offers sacrifice to God.

The great David, the courageous shepherd boy who stood up to Goliath, the mighty and fearsome Philistine warrior, conquered him with a skillful slingshot. David could not touch the Ark, because he was not a Levite as such, he was not a priest. The Jewish sacrifices did not achieve full absolution from sin and reconciliation with God. The author of Hebrews (9:14) calls them useless rituals. The Father achieved this infinite justice by having His Son, God by nature, empty Himself (Phil 2:7) thereby cleansing all who believe in His Son, once and for all (Heb 7:27). He remains God's high priest for all time.

As a result of the authority contained in Matt 16:18-20, Matt 18:18 and Luke 22:19, Jesus Christ requested His apostles, to renew the memorial of His New Covenant, sealed with His Own Body and Blood poured out for His Church. To accomplish this, The Church instituted the Sacrament of Holy Orders, establishing the ranks of Bishops, Priests and Deacons. Bishops and Priests have the authority to consecrate bread into the Body of Jesus Christ and wine into the Blood of Jesus Christ. When Jesus said "Whoever eats my flesh and drinks my blood has eternal life, and I will raise him to life on the last day. For my flesh is the real food, my blood is the real drink. Whoever eats my flesh and drinks my blood lives in me, and I live in him" (John 6:54-57). "Because of this, many of Jesus' followers turned back and would not go with him anymore. So He asked the twelve disciples, 'And you, would you also like to leave? Simon Peter answered Him, " Lord, to whom would we go? You have the words that give eternal life. And now we believe and know that you are the Holy One who has come from God" (John 6:66-70). What Jesus said and did is a mystery, and those of us who believe in this mystery achieve and continue to achieve a deep relationship and union with Jesus Christ. Subsequent to the consecration at Holy Mass, the ordained priest offers to the Father the Real Body and Real Blood of Jesus Christ and The Acceptable Sacrifice for His Church. This has been an on going Acceptable Sacrifice for His Church. Even though we, in our humanity, "Fall short," Romans 3:23, thanks to God's grace, the Church offers this on-going Acceptable Sacrifice.

The Eucharist was given by Jesus to the apostles and has been handed down to us by them and by their successors. Jesus said, "This is my body, which is given for you, do this in memory of Me" Luke 22:19. The Eucharist gives us a profoundly deep union with Jesus Christ and holds up the Church; in fact, through this mystery the Church comes into being. This dynamic interchange of sacramental grace will continue until the end times are achieved as expressed in 1 Cor. 15:24. "Then the end will come, Christ will over come all spiritual rulers, authorities, and powers and will hand over the Kingdom to God the Father." Then we will see the Lord Face to face and share in His Kingdom. Conditions for those who receive Holy Communion are that they have been baptized, that they have confessed, repented, and made a serious effort to reform from their sins, preferably with a priest through the sacrament of penance, and they believe they are receiving the Body and Blood of Jesus Christ. It is contrary to acceptable procedures to have inter-communion with Protestant denominations because we do not share the same doctrinal understanding. Yet under very serious conditions, Holy Communion can be given to a non-Catholic if he or she complies with the conditions outlined in Canon 844.

Jesus Christ gives us three forms of nourishment that enable us to become His Father's sons and daughters by grace: "My food is to do the Will of My Father and complete My mission" (John 4:34); "Man does not live by bread alone but by every word that comes from the mouth of God" (Dt 8:3, Mt/Lk 4:4); "Unless you eat My body, you will not have My life in you (Jn 6:53); My body is real food and my blood is real drink (Jn 6:55)." In response to this last, some of His followers said, "This teaching is too hard. Who can believe it (Jn 6:60)?" Yet Peter said, "Where do we go, He has the words of everlasting life (Jn 6:68)." Jesus said, "Do this (give His body and blood to one another in Holy Communion) in memory of Me (Lk22:19)." Only ordained priests have the authority to call on the Holy Spirit to change the bread and wine into the Body and Blood of Christ, just as only the Levites had the authority to touch the Ark. If we all had this authority; it would cause irreverence and reduce our faith in Christ's true presence.

Peter, in his first letter (2:19), said, "We are a royal priesthood." Paul asks us to "Offer ourselves (including those whom we have been asked to pray for and our loved ones) as a living sacrifice (Rom 12:1)." So, we, as ,Lay Priests,. participate in the most sublime contemplative prayer by connecting our "Living sacrifices" to THE HIGH PRIEST, Jesus Christ, and His once and for all sacrifice (Heb 7:27)Subsequent to the consecration at Mass during which time the priest requests the Holy Spirit to change bread into the body of Jesus Christ and wine into the blood of Jesus Christ., the priest then prays :We(I the ordained priest and you the lay priests,(1 Peter2:19)offer you, Father, this bread, now the body of Jesus Christ and wine now the blood of Jesus Christ, as an acceptable sacrifice connected to His original sacrifice, (Heab.7{27).This is our community sacrifice offered during all the Masses through the world.

In time, we receive Jesus Christ's body, yet Jesus Christ, timeless as God, transcends over two thousand years to the time of his crucifixion. Even though He has completed

His earthly mission, He joins our daily living sacrifices (Rom.12:1) and our community sacrifices with His once and for all sacrifice and presents these to His Father. Were we there? Not physically there. Yet our living sacrifices and our community were there,

We Christians have a tendency to be spectators, even in our worship for God. We are required to participate in Christ, through Christ, and with Christ in our worship of God. In 1 Corinthians 10:16 Paul tells us, "The Cup we use in the Lord's Supper and for which we give thanks to God: when we drink from it, we are sharing in the blood of Christ. And the bread we break: when we eat it we are sharing in the body of Christ."

Truly, this is the ultimate form of worship.

Worship is also mentioned in the Bible at:

Ex 20:3-6 Dt 5:7-9 Mt 4:10 Lm 4:8 Acts 10:22
Lv 10:3 Eccl 5:1-6 Ps 100 Prov 15:8 Rom 12:1

CHAPTER XV

Faith

"**M**y father has one work for you: that is believe in Me, the one He has sent (Mt 6:33 Jn. 6:29)." "Whoever believes in the Son is not judged; but whoever does not believe in Him has already been judged, because he does not believe in God's only Son (John 3:18)." "Those who do not believe in Me have condemned themselves (Mk 16:16)." It is clear that without faith in Jesus Christ, we cannot access His cleansing, His miraculous eternal life-giving energy, and love. In 1 Cor 13:12, Paul describes our perception of reality as a dim image in a mirror with partial knowledge, requiring faith. Yet, when we have the "Beatific vision," that is, see God face to face, we will have only love. Our virtues of faith and hope will no longer be required.

Faith in Christ is a beyond-comprehension power that enables us to, "move mountains (Matt 21:21)." So, in a real sense, before we achieve the "Beatific vision," we have a power that even angels do not have. We have faith in Jesus Christ – a faith that can make things happen. With faith in Jesus Christ, we are born to live. Without faith in Jesus

Christ, we are born to die. What about those who have never been introduced to Jesus Christ? What about the aborigines, the Hindus, Buddhists, the human fetus, and others like some of the Jews and Moslems who have never really been aware of Jesus Christ, or ever been given the opportunity of accepting and committing to Jesus Christ? The Father has more than the original common language computer skill; He can and does communicate with all of us without using language when He chooses to do so. Before any of us depart for eternity, the Father gives us our final choice. And all are given enough grace at some time in their lives to accept and believe in Jesus Christ (Rom 3:24 and 1 Tim 2:4). Do we choose His Son, Jesus Christ, the cleanser? Even at the last moment, if we choose Jesus Christ as the most important person in our life and commit to Him, as with St. Dismas (the "good thief") (Luke 23:42-44), Jesus brings us to the Father (John 14:6). However there may be some purgatory (1 Cor 3:15) along the way.

Further references to faith in Scripture can be found in:

Mk 9:24 Mt 17:20-21 John 1:50 Lk 12:22-29 Lk 7:50
John 14:27 Mt 9:22 Lk 11:28 Mk 16:16 John 6:29
John 3:16 Mark 11:23 Matt 21:21 Luke 7:23
Ephesians 2:8-9

Chapter XVI

Hope

Among our descriptions for God and His qualities, we always speak of His infinite hope and mercy (although He is also infinitely just – Ex 34:6-7). "I assure you that people can be forgiven of all their sins and all the evil things they may say. But whoever says evil things against the Holy Spirit will never be forgiven because he has committed an eternal sin (Mk 3:28-29)." As was mentioned, the Holy Spirit's mission is to give witness to Jesus Christ; so, when one intentionally "blocks out" the Holy Spirit, he is essentially eliminating faith in Christ Jesus, thereby condemning himself (Mk 16:16). "Everything written in Scriptures was written to teach us, in order that we might have hope through the patience and encouragement, which Scriptures give us (Rom 15:4)."

"Yet there was hope that creation itself would one day be set free from its slavery and would share the glorious freedom of the children of God. For we know that up to the present time, all of creation groans with pain, like the pain of childbirth. But it is not just creation alone which groans: we who have the Spirit as the first of God's gifts all groan within ourselves as we wait for God to make us His sons, by grace, and set our whole being free. For it was by hope that we were saved; but if we see what we hope for, then it is not really hope. For who hopes for something he sees? But if we hope for what we do not see, we wait for it with patience (Rom 8:20-25)." "For those who hope in the Lord will find their energy renewed. They will become energized (Is 40:31)."

Further references to hope can be found in:

Ps 31:24 Jer 14:22 Rom 15:13 Acts 24:15 1 Cor 15:19 Rom 5:5 2 Cor 3:12 Heb 3:6

CHAPTER XVII

Love

The most important aspect of God is His love, His infinite love. The object of all holy scripture is love. If we could put the love of everyone who has lived, is living, and will ever live into our heart, Jesus Christ still loves us more. He chose to empty Himself for us all (Phil 2:7). "The Father gave His only Son (by nature) to empty Himself so that everyone who believes in Him may not die but have eternal life (John 3:16)." Even when Jesus asked His Father to "Take this chalice from Me," the Father gave Him no reply. And when Jesus responded to the Father's silence with, "Not My Will but Yours be done," the Father sent an angel to His Son to strengthen and support Him (Lk 22:42-43).

Christ had two natures, human as well as divine. As a human, He had a brain, feelings, and choice. He knew He could have fulfilled all of the prophecies without having to suffer so much Himself. It was His humanity that prompted Him to ask His Father for the easier way. But the Father wanted no question about His love and the love of His Son and the Holy Spirit for all of us. He allowed His Son to give all as evidence of their unlimited love. The Holy Trinity had love for humanity from all eternity. "God is love (1 Jn 4:8)." "We love because God first loved us (1 Jn 4:19)." All of us, except the most unfortunate, have experienced love from others who are conduits of God's love, just as we are conduits of God's love for others. We should always consider the good and interest of others (1 Cor 10:24, 33).

To give influence, one should be like the person one is attempting to affect without compromising God's law. Regardless of how bad the person is we do have important things in common. We are all sinners, (the person who says he is not a sinner is a liar. (1 John 1:10). We all need and want more love, though many try for love the wrong way. We love because God first loves us (1 John 4:19). God is the source of love, (1 John 4:7 and 4:16) and only God can satisfy us with His unlimited love, which will compound for us throughout eternity (1 Corinthians 2:9 and Is 64:4). "What no one ever thought could happen, what no one ever saw or heard, is the very thing God prepares for those who love Him." We have an insight of how much God loves us by what the Son of God, Jesus Christ, has done for us. St. Augustine tells us that until we permanently experience God's love we humans remain restless.

In the incarnation, He emptied Himself for us (Phil 2:7). He became human except for sin (2 Cor 5:21). Though as human and the Son of man, Jesus Christ all the while remained the Son of God (Mark 14:61, Luke 10:18, John 8:28 and John 8:58). To atone for all our sins, He emptied Himself on the cross. He held back nothing. Water and blood came out when the spear was thrust into His side (John 19:34). Jesus Christ could have satisfied the prophesies in a much easier way, and still made redemption available for all of us. He even asked His Father for this concession (Luke 22:42) When His Father did not answer His request, He said, "Not My will but Yours be done." With incredible tension, "His sweat was like drops of blood falling to the ground (Luke 22:44)," He prayed deeply, reflecting on His own words, "My food is to obey the will of the one who sent me and to finish the work he gave me to do (John 4:34)." Why did not the Father consent to an easier way? The answer is eternal, unlimited and unconditional God's LOVE for all.

Many theologians believe He actually sweat blood. His Father then sent Him an angel to support Him. Why did not the Father consent to an easier way? I can never question whether God loves me. I can question it, but if I reflect on the question with a sincere heart, I will come to see that God does love me even if I cannot see it or understand it or feel it. Moreover, the Father has given us the right to become His adopted children, not because we are His creation and are born of parents, but because we accept and believe in His word, Jesus Christ (John 1:12). Though it appears not all of us accept and believe in His Word, God still wants all to be saved (1 Tim. 2:4). Therefore, God wants us to make intercessory prayer for all so that all can be saved (1 Tim. 2:1).

Further references to love in the Scriptures are:

Jn 5:39-42 Jn 16:27 Mt 10:37-39 Jn 15:12-17
Lk 6:32-33 Jn 15:9-11 Jn 17:24 Mt 5:43-45
Deut 7:7-10 and 12-13 Psalm 23 Isaiah 54
John 3:16 John 14:15 Romans 5:5 Eph 1:4-5 1
John 2:10 1 John 3:11 1 John 1:7-8 1 John 4:18-19
Luke 5:43-44 Deut 6:4-5 Lev 19:18 Matt 22:36-41

CHAPTER XVIII

Forgiveness

A definition of God is that He is all merciful yet all just (Exod. 34:6). In Exodus 32, when Moses came down from the mountain with the ten commandment tablets the Lord had given him, he saw his people worshipping the Golden Calf. He was angry. He broke the commandment tablets. He returned to God on the mountain. God was more angry than Moses and intended to eliminate all his chosen people, except Moses whom He would choose as one like Abraham.

Moses made the great intercessory prayer and requested God not eliminate these people. "Your enemies will think you brought them into the desert to get rid of them (Exod. 32:12)." Then God consented not to kill all the people at that time, yet He would not forget and He would eventually punish them for their sin. With God's justice, there had to be the consequence for their sin.

Yet Jeremiah prophesized in his 31:31-34 that God would establish a new covenant, not one of circumcision, but one of love and that he would choose to forgive and forget. In

Malachi 3:6, "God does not change." This appears that God does change. How could Jeremiah's prophecy be fulfilled in God's justice? His Son, Jesus Christ with his blood, achieved God's justice for all who would believe in Him. John 3:16, "For God loved the world so much that He gave His only Son, so that everyone who believes in him may not die, but have eternal life," so that all who believe in Jesus Christ and confess, repent, reform and forgive others are forgiven. Even though everything we express is recorded, (Matt 12:36), the Lord chooses to forgive and forget (Heb. 10:17).

In Mark 3:29, Jesus said all sins can be forgiven except the sin against the Holy Spirit. This means that when the Holy Spirit is "blocked out" during the "violation of God's law," the Spirit's gift of faith (1 Cor 12:9) is also "blocked out." Without faith in Jesus Christ, we condemn ourselves (Mk 16:16). The question naturally appears, what about those who practice different religions that do not believe in Jesus Christ? And what about the souls of those like aborted human fetuses who have never known Jesus Christ? God wants us all to be saved (1 Tim 2:4). God does not have to lecture, preach, or use understandable language to communicate. As God, He has and does communicate with the intellect of the soul directly without using words. What is required is that the will of the soul respond positively, by choosing God's Redeemer, the One Isaiah predicted will come to make people whole and cleansed (Is 53:6). Because we are all conceived and born in sin, we need the Savior otherwise known as the Messiah, God's Son, Jesus Christ. "I was conceived and born in sin and need to be cleansed (PS 51:1,5)." Furthermore, God gives all of us enough grace to make the right choice (Rom 3:24). Jesus Christ said, "I come to help the sinners not the self-righteous (Mt 9:13)." So those who feel they have not violated God's law in any way are self-righteous and appear to be in trouble, because the Messiah did not come for them. He came as a physician for those who need and want Him (Mk 2:17). We are all sinners, "The person who says he is not a sinner is a liar (1 Jn 1:10)." Yet when we confess our sins, which include repentance and reformation, we are forgiven (1 Jn 1:9). The "good thief," Dismas, publicly confessed his sins when he said, "We are getting what we deserve for what we did (Lk 23:41)." Incidentally, his honesty cleared the way for God's grace, which enabled him to express his belief in Jesus Christ and be saved, "I promise you, this day you will be in Paradise with Me (Lk 34:43)."

In what manner can and should the rest of us confess our sins? In James (5:16), "Confess your sins to one another." The Lord wants a serious admission of our sins and that we "Go and sin no more (Jn 8:11)." Catholics are blessed to have the sacrament of reconciliation (confession) wherein the priest, under the seal of confidentiality and silence, acts with the authority as the agent of Jesus Christ. "Whose sins you shall forgive, they are forgiven (Mt 16:19)."

Contained in the prayer Jesus Himself gave us, the Our Father, as we ask for forgiveness, we are required to forgive others (Mt 6:12). How often should we forgive others? Jesus told Peter, "70 times 70 (Mt 18:22)." When Jesus told the paralyzed man lying on the bed, "Courage my son. Your sins are forgiven," some of the teachers of the law, said to him, "This man is speaking blasphemy." Jesus responded with, "Why are you thinking these evil thoughts? Is it easier to say, 'get up and walk,' or to say 'your sins are forgiven?' I will prove to you that the son of Man has the authority on earth to forgive sins." He then said, "Arise and pick up your bed and walk home (Mt 9:2-6)."

Further references to forgiveness in the Bible are:

Jn 8:3-12 Lk 17:3-4 Mk 3:28-29 Mt 9:12-13
Mt 12:31 Lk 23:39-44 Mt 6:14-15 Lk 7:4-7

CHAPTER XIX

Judgment

"The Father has given His Son the full right to judge, so that all will honor the Son in the same way as they honor the Father. Whoever does not honor the Son does not honor the Father (Jn 5:22-23)." "I can do nothing on my own authority; I judge only as God tells Me, so My judgment is right because I am not trying to do what I want, but only what He who sent me wants (Jn 5:30)." Conversely, Jesus said, "Judge not and you shall not be judged (Mt 7:1)."

"A healthy tree bears good fruit, but a poor tree bears bad fruit. You will know them by what they do (Mt 7:17-20)." So, Jesus expects us to be "fruit inspectors," which is different from standing in judgment on another. In Luke 17:3, as Jesus tells us, "If your brother or sister sins, rebuke him or her." So, there is a major distinction between judging another and identifying the breaking of God's law, which is sin (1 Jn 3:4) and rebuking it. Jesus goes further when He says, "If your brother sins against you, go to him and show him his fault. But do it privately, just between yourselves. If he listens to you, you won your brother back. But if he will not listen to you, take one or two others with you, so that every accusation may be reasonably witnessed. And if he will not listen to them, tell the whole thing to the church (Mt 18:15-17)," and put him on the prayer list because, "We should pray for all so that all can be saved (1 Tim 2:1-4)."

Furthermore, Jesus did give details about the final judgment. "When the Son of Man comes as King and all the angels with Him, He will sit on His royal throne, and the people of all nations will be gathered before Him. Then He will divide them into two groups, just as a shepherd separates the sheep from the goats. He will put the righteous people at his right and the others at His left (Mt 25:31-33)." He proceeds with details about the good works of the righteous and the neglect of good works by the others, "Who will be sent off to eternal punishment (Is.66:24andMk.9:48), while the righteous will go to eternal life (Mt 25:46)." However, in Romans (3:27), Paul warns us we can boast of nothing; yet, in James (2:17), it is said, "Faith without good works is dead."

Other references to judgment in Scripture include:

Mt 25:31-46 Mt 23:23 Lk 6:24-26 Lk 11:34-36
Lk 6:37-39 Mk 13:24-27 Lk 19:42-44 Jn 5:24
Lk 15:7 Mk 16:16

CHAPTER XX

Consequences

It is a common topic to think about rights. The American Civil Liberties Union (ACLU) has made it clear we all have rights. The media has supported the ACLU's position that we all have many rights. Yet for every right, there is a corresponding responsibility to respect the right of others. It appears that neither the media nor the ACLU have promoted this principle. It appears that they have promoted "Pro choice" without consequence. The consequence of our choice is basic, yet you would never know it the way the ACLU and the media promote the importance of our choice and rights.

Without going to school, we learn early about gravity and water, and the tragic consequences of the misuse of these two elements of nature. God is the author of nature. You cannot separate God from nature. As with tragic physical consequences with the misuse of nature, there are tragic spiritual consequences with the misuse and violation of God's laws. "Whoever sins is guilty of breaking God's law (1 John 3:4)." "For sin pays its wage-death (Romans 6:23)." When we selfishly choose such as killing someone who obstructs our interests, as in abortions, or steal from someone by misrepresenting value or have sex out of marriage (Mark 7:21-24), OR VIOLATING ANY OTHER OF THE Ten Commandments (Exodus 20:1-17), we break God's law, which is sin, and our consequence is death.

Our spiritual life does have direct influence over our physical life in a psychosomatic manner. So when a person violates God's law, which is sin, and receives a death result from the spirit, the soul, it achieves a negative physical consequence. As God permits nature consequences, He also permits spiritual consequences, hell (Isaiah 66:24 and Mark 9:48). Christ's parable about the Kingdom of Heaven with the king who prepared a wedding feast for his son from Matt 22:1-14, helps clarify compliance requirements for salvation and admission into heaven. The king observed a guest without a wedding garment on (wedding garments were routinely given for guests in Christ's day), and questioned him why he had not put one on. The person was silent and gave no answer. So the king ordered his servants to tie him up hand and foot, and throw him outside in the dark. There he will cry and gnash his teeth (Matt 22:13). Those who do not comply with God's requirements, that is those who do not accept God's grace and have faith in Jesus Christ have condemned themselves (Ephes 2:8-9 and Mark 16:16). The consequence of the person rejecting God's grace and choosing not to believe in Jesus Christ, results in God putting him in hell (Luke 12:4-6).

Hell is the eternal consequence for people who are selfish and choose pleasures and self interest as their priority Those people even without intent, have indirectly connected with Satin. He is the father of lies. He accuses ourselves, our brothers, and sisters of our sins, and how we've fallen short. Day and night,(Rev.12:10)&Rom.3:23).With his hate, he kills people before their providential life concludes.(Psalm118:

17)Regrettably, many people experience real evidence off hell before their physically die. However the certain reality of hell exists with the Satin and being subject to him in his company for eternity .

Yet ,what the Father intended for all is to receive His unlimited love compounded through eternity(Tim.1:4) As in the song's fifth verse of AMAZING GRACE, Though we've been there 10,000 years we .are still praising the Lord." How can anyone do something for 10,000 years without being board ? Does anyone ever get board with love? The Father supplements His love with wisdom, understanding knowledge and discernment which also compounds throughout eternity There we have it. The consequence of our dedicated choice is endlessly compounded: LOVE,JOY AND PEACE.

CHAPTER XXI

Salvation

W hat does Jesus Christ say we are saved from? Without faith in Jesus Christ and in rebellion against God, one is thrown into hell. By rejecting God's grace and refusing to believe in Jesus Christ, people choose this consequence. This is what we should fear (Lk 12:4). "There, the worms that eat them never die, and the fire that burns them is never put out (Mk 9:47-48)." In this manner, Jesus quoted Isaiah's last chapter and verse, 66:24. Revelation (21:8) describes the eternal lake burning with fire and sulfur. However, those who have become God's sons and daughters through grace, that is, being born of water and the Holy Spirit (Jn 3:5) and by accepting, believing, dedicating and consecrating themselves to Jesus Christ are saved (Jn 1:12, 17:17, Pt 3:15). Paul says this result is guaranteed by the Holy Spirit (2 Cor 5:5).

Physically, we are born to die. Spiritually, we are born to live. Jesus said, "My kingdom does not belong to this world; otherwise, my servants (angels) would fight to keep Me from being handed over to the Jewish authorities (Jn 18:36)." Some Pharisees asked Jesus when the Kingdom of God would come. Jesus answered that, "The Kingdom of God does not come in such a way as to be seen. No one will say look, here it is, or there it is, because the Kingdom of God is within you (Lk 17:21)." So, in that manner, Jesus tells us that those who are sons and daughters by grace are already participating in His Kingdom. In Revelation 21, John records his visions that describe what the new heaven and new earth will be like. In 1 Cor 15, Paul describes Jesus Christ's resurrection and the future resurrection of God's sons and daughters by grace. Paul predicts in 1 Cor 15:24, subsequent to Jesus' second coming, "Then, the end will come; Christ will overcome all spiritual rulers, authorities, and powers and will hand over the Kingdom to God the Father." It should be noted that Paul paraphrases Isaiah (64:4), describing God's Kingdom as, "What no one ever saw or heard, what no one ever thought could happen is the very thing God prepares for those who love Him (1 Cor 2:9)." And Jesus assured us in John (14:2) that, "There are many rooms in My Father's house and I am going to prepare a place for you."

Further biblical references concerning salvation are:

Lk 19:9-10 Jn 3:16-17 Jn 17:3 Mt 18:12-14
Lk 18:29-30 Jn 11:25-26 Mt 10:40-42 Jn 16:20-23
Lk 23:39-43

CHAPTER XXII

Discernment of Spirits

"But I am telling you the truth: it is better for you that I go away, because if I do not go, the Helper will not come to you. But if I do go away, then I will send Him to you. And when He comes, He will prove to the people of the world that they are wrong about sin and about what is right and about God's judgment. They are wrong about sin, because I am going to the Father and you will not see me anymore; and they are wrong about judgment, because the ruler of this world has already been judged" (John 16:7-16). Jesus Christ did as He said He would do (Lk. 18:33). He did go away, that is He suffered, He died, He arose from the dead, and He ascended into heaven. He completed His mission; and only after this could the Holy Spirit come to give complete witness for Jesus Christ. This historical event is known as Pentecost (Greek word for fifty days after Christ's resurrection). The Holy Spirit came at Pentecost to give the Apostles, disciples, and followers of Jesus Christ His gifts (1 Cor. 12:8-10) and His fruits (Gal 5:22-24) which would help them become more bold, confident and skilled in giving better witness for Jesus Christ, thereby implementing the Holy Spirit's own mission. Discernment is one of the gifts the Holy Spirit gave Jesus Christ's followers. Discernment is clear thinking and recognizing distinctions to achieve clear thoughts. It can help one see things as they really are by recognizing the voice of God and what He is asking of us at this time in our lives. "Do not put the Lord your God to the test" Deut. 6:16. We don't test the Lord, yet the Lord permits us to be tested. In the Book of Job the Lord permitted Satan to take Job's assets away resulting in a test of how real was Job's dedication and love relationship for God. After Job's assets were taken away, Job's comment was, "I was born with nothing, and I will die with nothing. The Lord gave, and now he has taken away. May his name be praised!" (Job 1:21) This did not satisfy Satan. He asked for permission from God to take away Job's health. Permission was given. Then Job was visited and criticized for having done something wrong by his three acquaintances. What else could have caused Job's condition? (Jeremiah 7:23), "But I did command them to obey me, so that I would be their God and they would be my people. And I told them to live the way I had commanded them, so that things would go well for them." In a frustrated moment Job asked the Lord why he received these afflictions. And God responded to Job, "Who are you to question my wisdom." (Job 38:2) Elsewhere in Hosea 11:9 God says, "For I am God and not man." Job then told God he was sorry for having questioned Him. (Job 42:6), and after Job made an intercessory prayer for his three acquaintances (God wants us to forgive and pray for those whom we forgive) God returned health to Job and doubled his former assets. (Job 42:10)

Why did God permit Job to be afflicted? "My son, pay attention when the Lord corrects you, and do not be discouraged when he rebukes you. Because the Lord corrects everyone he loves, and punishes everyone he accepts as a son." (Hebrew 12:6 and Job 5:17) Also the Lord says, "My thoughts are not like yours, and my ways are different from yours." (Isaiah 55:8)

How often have we tasted something good with a sick stomach result? How often have we experienced much consolation with a regrettable result? Conversely, how often have we experienced no consolation in our activities with some good and productive results? It is natural to want good feelings and consolation contained in our work and relationships, yet those feelings can be very misleading. Then how can we be sure our judgments are correct? With the Holy Spirit's gift of discernment we can prove whether our judgments are correct or not. Our, "Litmus" test is whether Jesus Christ remains number one in our priorities or has He been relegated to a second rate priority, and has our judgment been in compliance with God's word in Holy Scripture. If our judgment satisfies this test we are at least 51% correct and more probably 100% correct. If our judgment is not 100% correct we should do as Jesus Christ did. He prayed for hours. Why did He have to pray for so many hours? Jesus Christ is human as we are except for sin (2 Cor. 5:21) yet He is also God, the begotten Son of God. As such He knows all things. Yet as human, he had to reconcile His judgments to what His Father wanted. If Jesus Christ needed to pray so much, should not we have to pray more? When we pray with courage, perseverance and faith, the "Light" turns on eventually. We have certainty in our conclusions.

We all have a natural tendency to want "feed-back" from our relationships about how we have achieved. Have we passed the test? Have we been recognized for our efforts? Most frequently we get the best "feed-back" from the Holy Spirit. When we have done good things, the Holy Spirit gives us His LOVE, JOY AND PEACE "Feed-Back." We do not test God, but we do test the spirit. Is it the good spirit or the bad spirit? An excellent Scripture support in helping with this test is contained in 1 John 5:1-13. Furthermore, discernment requires an objectivity that cannot always be achieved by one's own personal effort. "Get advice and you will succeed." (Prov. 20:18) "Get all the advice you can and you will succeed." (Prov. 15-22). Objectivity can be assisted by confession. "Confess your sins to one another." (James 5:16) We Catholics have the privilege of confessing our violation of God's laws, defined as sin in 1 John 3:4, to a priest with absolute confidentiality. In this confession dialogue we can achieve more objectivity and confidence that our sins are forgiven by God through the sacramental absolution of the priest.

CHAPTER XXIII

Call To Holiness

"I am the Lord your God, you must keep yourselves holy, because I am holy." (Leviticus 11:44) 1 Peter 3:15 supports this request. The Gideon Society since 1899 adds to this reference. It says that when you consecrate and dedicate yourself to the Lord, you become holy.

What is holiness? Isaiah wrote, "We are healed by the punishment he suffered, made whole by the blows he received." (53:5) A synonym for wholeness is integrity. (The Webster's New World Dictionary, College Edition, with a copyright of 1959). In Genesis 8, Noah offered a sacrifice to the Lord in thanksgiving for his and his family's survival from the Flood. In Genesis 9:8-14, "God said to Noah and his sons, "I am now making my covenant with you and your descendents, and with all living beings – all birds and all animals – everything that came out of the boat with you. With these words I make my covenant with you: I promise that never again will a flood destroy the earth. As a sign of this everlasting covenant, which I am making with you and with all living beings, I am putting my bow in the clouds. It will be the sign of my covenant with the world." Contained in this covenant was Noah's relationship to God. He and his family were required to continue to praise, reverence and serve God by keeping His commandments. Also contained in this covenant was Noah's relationship with his family and all eventual humanity. Finally contained in this covenant was Noah's relationship with all of God's creation including animals, vegetables, minerals, the earth and its atmosphere. Through time the great saints, notably St. Francis of Assisi, have always had a deep integral connection with these three relationships. In other words they had a condition of integrity resulting in holiness. The very sign of this first covenant was the rainbow, which contains the colors of the spectrum in consecutive bands, a perfect vision of integrity. The virtue of integrity is always admired and Christians as a group should excel in it. What is the most direct contribution to integrity? It is Love. So by improving our love for God and for our neighbor, especially for "the least important of Jesus Christ's brothers," (Matt. 25:40), we improve our integrity. And while doing so, we fulfill the TWO GREAT COMMANDMENTS: (Deut. 6:5, Lev. 19:34, Lev. 19:18 and Matt 22:37-41). We should love others as Jesus Christ has loved us (John 15:12). Love drives out fear and perfect love eliminates fear (1 John 4:18).

Those who love the Lord trust in the Lord. "You have made the Lord your defender, the Most High your protector, and so no disaster will strike you, no violence will come near your home. God will put his angels in charge of you to protect you wherever you go. They will hold you up with their hands to keep you from hurting yourself"(Psalms 91:9-12). God says, "I will save those who love me and will protect those who acknowledge me as Lord. When they call to me, I will answer them: when they are in trouble, I will be with them" (Psalms 91:14, 15). Those who love and trust in the Lord, will not fear another "9/11." We are required to plan our work and work our plan, and then does God's providence take over (Prov. 16:9). Those who love the Lord trust in His providence, because His providence contains an infinite amount of love for us, and He will provide for our important needs in a better way than we would do so for ourselves. Love, fruit of the Holy Spirit, contributes to trust in God, integrity, and holiness and "Peace that the world cannot give" (John 14:27). Whereas a condition without love, contributes to distrust, anger, hate, and an attitude that results in, "A life for a life, an eye for an eye, a tooth for a tooth, a hand for a hand and a foot for a foot" (Deuteronomy 19:21).

CHAPTER XXIV

A Definition of God

"I, the Lord, am a God who is full of compassion and pity, who is not easily angered and who shows great love and faithfulness. I keep my promise for thousands of generations and forgive evil and sin; but I will not fail to punish children and grandchildren to the third and fourth generation for sins of their parents!" (Exodus 34:6&7) We see examples and exceptions to God's punishment throughout history. A good example of an exception is St. Francis Borgia, third General of the Society of Jesus Jesuit Order. He overcame his Borgia family influence and became a saint. Simplified, this definition of God is that He is all just yet all merciful. His manner of justice and mercy is beyond our understanding. "My thoughts, says the Lord, are not like yours, and my ways are different from yours. As high as the heavens are above the earth, so high are my ways and thoughts above yours" (Isaiah 55:8&9). "For I am God and not man" (Hosea 11:9).

In civil and equity law, the judge gives a sentence to those who violate the law. In a similar way with a completely different manner, God gives a sentence to those who do not comply with His plan. "Do not be afraid of those who kill the body but cannot kill the soul; rather be afraid of God, who can destroy both body and soul in hell" (Matt. 10:28). "Whoever believes in the Son is not judged; but whoever does not believe has already been judged, because he has not believed in God's only Son." (John 3:18) As in Mark 16:16 those who choose not to believe in Jesus Christ have condemned themselves. Yet it is God, The Judge, Who puts them in hell. (Luke 12:4) However, God gives grace for all to be saved. "But by the free gift of God's grace all are put right with Him through Christ Jesus, who sets them free." (Romans 3:24) When a person sins by intentionally violating God's law, or by his addictions he continues to sin, how can he access God's mercy and reconnect with God's grace? He must first confess his sins and repent, reform and forgive others, as in the OUR FATHER prayer. "But if we confess our sins to God, He will keep His promise and do what is right: He will forgive us our sins and purify us from all our wrong doing." (1 John 1:9) In confession, The Lord requires us to choose to be forgiven with a sincere heart. As a result of the original sin, we have a tendency in our heart to seek the wrong objectives with our wrong priorities. Our greed has a tendency to make dull our judgments. (Prov. 23:3) We seek after what is false and love what is worthless. (Psalm 4:2) We are deceived by flattery and have less respect for the truth. (Psalm 12 & 36:1) Our pride has deceived us. (Jer. 49:16) Pride of heart leads to destruction. (Prov. 16:18) It is the pride of our heart causing foolishness to limit our judgments within our own opinions. (Prov. 28:26) And our pride of heart results in the ultimate condition of foolishness in denying God, becoming corrupt and our ultimate self-destruction. (Psalm 14:1&53:1) "I will not tolerate a man who is proud and arrogant." (Psalm 101:5)

When we fulfill our baptism by dedicating and conse-crating ourselves to Jesus Christ, we access the cleansing of our hearts by the fulfillment of Isaiah's prophecy contained in His entire 53rd Chapter. Jesus Christ has cleansed the hearts of us who believe in Him and have loved Him with our whole heart, intellect and will. With a clean heart we are destined to see God. (Matt. 5:8) How can we retain this pure heart? We should develop the characteristics of clear conscience (Gen. 20:5) unselfish devotion to good works (Psalms 78:72 & James 2:17), serving God with honesty and integrity (1 Kings 9:4), develop a humble and repentant heart (Psalms 51:17), deny ourselves bad habits and passions of youth (2 Tim 2:22), and ask the lord for help to achieve a pure heart (Psalms 51:10). We should also perform regular spiritual exercises: prayer (Luke 21:36), hearing and reading Holy Scripture (Romans 10:17), fellowship with good Christian people, (1 John 1:3), good works (James 2:17), fasting (Mark 2:20) and tithing (Malachi 3:10). We should also recite and fulfill (all for Jesus) our daily morning offering. Yet with all these efforts, we still fall short (Romans 3:23), and are sinners (1 John 1:10). When we confess our sins we are forgiven (1 John 1:9). We are required to confess our sins to one another (James 5:16). As a Catholic, we have the privilege of confessing to a priest in sacramental confession. As a person who needs insurance would reasonably get insurance from an insurance agent instead of going directly to the insurance company, we Catholics would rather go to God's agent, the priest, than go directly to God. The insurance agent has the authority to discuss the details of the insurance contract and bind the insurance benefits, giving the insured his peace of mind with his required guarantees. The priest has the authority to confidentially hear the confession, discuss the details of God's laws and how they may have been broken, and give absolution for the sins on condition that the penitent has confessed all his recent sins, sincerely repented of them, resolved to sin no more (John 8:11), and make restitution for the wrongs he caused for others. The priest gives "penance," things to do or prayers to say, as a kind of partial restitution to God for his sins and as a sign of commitment to change.

God is all merciful. His mercy is unlimited. Yet He requires honesty. We are made in His image (Gen 1:26) with the ability to choose to recognize our violation of God's laws, or to justify these violations for personal reasons. Before we can access His mercy we must admit our sins (1 John 1:9). God's mercy for them is uncertain. We cannot know the mind of God (Isaiah 55:8&9) nor can we presume to know the state of grace of others before God. Jesus Christ came to serve and save and not to judge (John 3:17). Incidentally, He will be given the authority to judge, separating the "sheep from the goats" (Matt. 25:40). We too are forbidden to judge (Matt 7:1). Without question, the Lord wants all to be saved. (1 Tim 2:4) And the Lord wants us to make intercessory prayers for all so that even those of the most hardened hearts will open their hearts for God's grace, and confess their sins, repent and reform their lives, and as a result, receive God's mercy and be saved.

CHAPTER XXV

Christian Response to World Conscience

The dictionary definition of conscience is the faculty by which distinctions are made between moral right and wrong, especially in regard to one's own conduct; moral discrimination. The Catholic Encyclopedia on CD-Rom, expressed in www.google.com has given twenty-two pages of information for 'conscience.' In a most precise manner this Catholic Encyclopedia subdivides this word into the following topics: Origin of Conscience in the Human Race and in the Individual, What Conscience is in the Soul of Man. The Philosophy of Conscience considered historically, Conscience determined by Christian Fathers, The Platonic Consideration of Conscience, the Scholastic consideration of Conscience, The Anti-Scholastic consideration of Conscience including Spinoza, and Hobbes and, The Practical Working of Conscience, Education and Perfectibility of Conscience and The Approvals and Reapprovals of Conscience. St.

Thomas in his Summa Theologica is generally accepted as a reasonable authority for understanding the Soul of man.

In his question number 76 contained in the first part of his Summa Theologica Article #13, he questions whether Conscience is a Power of the Soul. Origin says that conscience is, "A correcting and guiding spirit accompanying the soul, by which it is led away from evil and made to cling to good." He and some other Christian Fathers believed conscience is a power of the soul. St. Thomas said Conscience can be laid aside but a power of the soul cannot be laid aside. For Conscience, according to the very nature of the word implies the relation of knowledge to something. The application of knowledge to something is done by some act. Conscience is said to witness, to bind, or stir up, and also to accuse, torment, or rebuke. All these things follow the application of knowledge to what we do. Conscience dominates the act, but since habit is a principle of act, sometimes the name conscience is given to the first natural habit-namely, synderesis: thus Jerome calls synderesis conscience.

St. Augustine in his DeTrin xii says that synderesis seems the same as reason, and therefore a power. Yet St. Thomas says that rational powers regard opposite things. Synderesis does not regard opposites, but inclines to good only. Synderesis is a natural habit. In his subject on Free Choice (Article 2) contained in question 83 of his Summa Theologica, he says that Free Choice is an additional power of the soul, because free choice is the subject of God's Grace, by which it chooses what is good. Incidentally, in the book of Genesis 1:24 we are all made in His image with a 'free choice.'

As the individual has his or her own fingerprint and DNA, he or she has their own unique Conscience. This unique conscience is formed by habit (synderesis) with free choice to do what it perceives as good. So, every person, who has lived and will live, has their own unique and different conscience.

The last request Jesus Christ gave us before He ascended into Heaven was, "Go, then, to all peoples everywhere and make them my disciples: baptize them in the name of the Father, the Son, and the Holy Spirit, and teach them to obey everything I have commanded you." (Mt. 28:19 & 20) What is Baptism? It is an outward sign instituted by God to give Grace. (Old penny catechism) To whom is baptism given? It is given to children and infants of parents (Acts 16:33) who have promised to give serious Christian formation to their children. Baptism is also given to adults and youth who have promised to dedicate and consecrate themselves to Jesus Christ. Dedicating themselves to Christ by putting Him as number one in their lives and Consecrating themselves to Jesus Christ by choosing to avoid bad company (1Cor. 5:9) and seek out good company (1Jn1:3). Once baptized, the person should continue to dedicate and consecrate himself to Jesus Christ (1v11:44) enabling himself to fulfill his Baptism and become holy. By doing this, one contributes to his Christian formation by developing good habits and spiritual exercises (prayer, bible reading and hearing, Christian fellowship, good works, fasting and tithing, all with scriptural authorized references). Thereby the person develops his good conscience assisting him to seek and do good.

What about the majority of people in the world who neither knows nor believes in Jesus Christ nor chooses to comply with His commandments? How should a Christian relate to these people? We are all required to give witness for Jesus Christ to all whom in some way we connect with. All Christians have authority to baptize non-Christians. Yet before Baptism is achieved serious Christian formation should be given. We Catholics and some Protestants have good pre-baptism programs and we should all encourage them. Yet we Christians should do more. St. Paul tells us 2Ti4:3 "The time will come when people will not listen to sound doctrine, but will follow their own desires and will collect for themselves more and more teachers who will tell them what they are itching to hear. They will turn away from listening to the truth and give their attention to legends. But you must keep control of yourself in all circumstances, endure suffering, do the work of a preacher of the Good News and perform your whole duty as a servant of God." 2Ti4:3-6. How can a lay, unordained Christian preach in this way? He should do as the Word of God has told him Ro8:14. The Holy Spirit will tell him what to say, how to say it, and when to say it Mt10:19. If the Christian is not inspired what to do or say, let his conduct (EPH 5:8) be the appropriate rebuke Lk17:3. And throughout this Evangelistic adventure, the Christian should be led by the Holy Spirit Ro8:26 in making intercessory prayer (1Ti2:1) for the convert. To perform in this manner, it is essential to be connected with the Holy Spirit. Our six spiritual exercises and our daily morning offering containing dedication and consecrating ourselves to Jesus Christ will help us connect with the Holy Spirit. The Holy Spirit's mission is to give witness for Jesus Christ (Jn16:7 & Rev 19:10). When the Holy Spirit identifies a person who daily dedicates and consecrates himself to Christ and supports this offering with his spiritual exercises, The Holy Spirit perceives this person as an implement for His mission, and gives this person His additional Gifts & Fruits so that he can be more bold, skilled and effective in giving witness for Christ.

The new Pope Benedict 16th described the major evil in the world today is RELATIVISM: That is one person's perception about truth is as real as another person's perception about truth. In other words, Truth is subjective. St. Thomas Aquinas in his Summa Theologica gives us clear thinking about Truth with his syllogisms. An example of this is all men are mortal, John is a man; therefore, John is mortal. St. Thomas wrote, beyond the capability of human "clear thinking," we need God's help to enable us to arrive at full and complete Truth. St. Thomas said God has given us this method to arrive at Total Truth with His Revelation contained in the Bible. The word contained in the Bible is Jesus Christ (Rev. 19:13 and John 1:1-5). We can prove our conclusions to the Truth are correct if they comply with the messages contained in scripture and that Jesus Christ, The Word, remains number one in our priorities. Our conclusions are his Father's will.

Though the word of God is Jesus Christ (Rev. 19:13), and Jesus Christ is the Truth (John 14:6), we should be cautious about interpreting God's word. (Our conclusions will probably not be 100% correct, yet no less than 51% correct. If there are any questions about our conclusions, we should do as Jesus Christ did. He prayed hours to reconcile Himself to His Father's will). "Above all else, however, remember that no one can explain by himself a prophecy in the Scripture. For no prophetic message ever came just from the will of man, but men were under the control of the Holy Spirit as they spoke the message that came from God" (2 Peter 1:20 & 21). This is what he (Paul) says in all his letters when he writes on the subject (of salvation). There are some difficult things in his letters, which ignorant and unstable people explain falsely, as they do with other passages of the Scriptures. "So they bring on their own destruction" (2 Peter 3:16).

We have an example with Jesus Christ Himself, who was human, though never sinned (2 Cor. 5:21), and who was God (Luke 10:18). "I saw Satan fall" (John 8:28 & 58) and "I Am Who I Am." And in Mark 14:62 Jesus Christ admitted He was the begotten Son of God. Jesus Christ, as human, had to reconcile Himself to His Father's will with the assistance of long prayers. In addition to our prayers, we have His church represented by the Pope and the ordained clergy. In Matt 16:18 & 19, He gave Peter and His Church authority that what they bind on earth will be bound in Heaven. In matters of faith and morals, the Popes contained in the historical Catholic Church have always complied with God's word in Scripture.

Conclusion

The final thing Jesus told His apostles to do was to return to Jerusalem, and wait for the Holy Spirit who will prepare and lead them with the assistance of His gifts and fruits (1 Cor 12:8-10 and Gal 5:22) to go throughout the world and give witness on behalf of Jesus Christ (Luke 24:47-50). We too are required to give witness for Jesus Christ, but as with the apostles, we are required to wait for the Holy Spirit's gifts and fruits to assist us in our witness for Christ. "The Holy Spirit will teach us all things (John 16:13)," and "He will tell us what to say and how to say it and when to say it (Matt 10:18)." He guarantees results for ourselves and for the others we witness to (2 Cor 5:5).

More basically, with so many religious methods to choose from, do the Christians have the only solution for salvation? What about good people throughout the ages who never either knew Jesus Christ nor appeared to believe in Him? With the Father's love and mercy, should not they achieve salvation? Only God can completely understand the heart of people. "Where your heart is, there your treasure is (Matt 6:21)." Simply putting it, The Father has a plan, which became effective after our "first parents" violated God's law, which is sin (1 John 3:4). Genesis 3, His plan is to have all people saved, (1 Tim 2:4) with an essential condition that they believe in His Son Jesus Christ. "One work My Father has for you, that you believe in Me His Son (John 6:29)." No one can come to the Father except through Me. I am the life, the truth, and the way to the Father (John 14:6)." What about the many good people who have prayed and fasted well, and have done good works? Should not they be acceptable for the Father? The Great courageous David who over came Goliath and who wrote God's inspired psalms said, "I was conceived and born in sin (Psalm 51:6)." And, "I need to be cleansed (Psalm 51:1)." If David was affected and under the influence of "original sin," our first parents' sin, who of us can think we were not affected by "original sin" and do not need cleansing? We all need to be cleansed. "I will send My suffering Servant to make you whole and cleanse you (Isaiah 51:6)." This person that Isaiah prophesized about is Jesus Christ, The Father's Son. Everyone needs "The Cleanser," Jesus Christ in order to enter into the Father's presence.

Everyone is given enough grace to eventually make this all-important choice (Romans 3:24). The Father can communicate the necessary grace to all and receive the essential response from all without using a given vernacular. Having given His Son as the Slain Lamb (Rv 12:11), He certainly wants all to be saved (1 Tim 2:4) Those of us who believe and love Jesus Christ and comply with His commands (John 14:15) are required to pray for all so that all can be saved (1 Tim 2:1). We should refrain from making any judgments about who will or who will not be saved (Matt 7:1). Yet Christ said that those who do not believe in Me have condemned themselves (Mark 16:16).

The Father's plan is that we should give witness for His Son Jesus and pray for all so that all can be saved (1 Tim 2:4). When the Father chooses to have authority, faith, power and obedience given to His Son Jesus, the final prophecy will be complete. Jesus Christ will then give all this power, obedience and authority to His Father and there will be love, joy and peace for His Family through eternity (1 Cor 15:28). However, between now and then, there remains pain and blood for us giving witness for Christ and His commandments.

Furthermore, in conclusion we are privileged beyond comprehension to have the entirety of God's revelation given to us in the form of the Bible, which is God's Word. "Your Word is a lamp to guide me and a light for my path (Psalm 119:105)." "Your message (Word) is like fire burning deep within me (Jeremiah 20:9)." "My message (Word) is like a fire and like a hammer that breaks rocks in pieces (Jer 23:29)." "And I told them to live the way I had commanded them (Live by My Word) so that things would go well for them (Jer 7:23)." "So then, faith comes from hearing the message (God's Word) Romans 10:17." Every word in the Bible is God's Word, which either directly or indirectly identifies, supports, and compliments the Messiah, as in the Old Testament, and Jesus Christ Who is the Messiah, as in the New Testament. The words and, "Truth that Jesus revealed is what inspired the prophets to give witness for the Messiah, Jesus Christ (Rev 19:10)."

Jeremiah writes in his 31:31-34, "The time is coming when I will make a new covenant with the people of Israel and with the people of Judah. It will not be like the old covenant that I made with their ancestors when I took them by the hand and led them out of Egypt. Although I was like a husband to them, they did not keep that covenant. The new covenant that I will make with the people of Israel will be this; I will put my law within them and write it on their hearts. I will be their God, and they will be my people. None of them will have to teach his fellow countryman to know the Lord, because all will know Me from the least to the greatest. I will forgive their sins and I will no longer remember their wrongs. I, the Lord have spoken."

"The definition of God is that He is all merciful, and yet all just (Ex 34:6)." When Moses broke the tablets containing the ten commandments because Aaron and his people were worshipping a golden calf, and returned to the mountain and made an intercessory prayer for his people for God's forgiveness, God relented from His intent to annihilate His people, but said, "The time is coming when I will punish these people for their sin (Ex 32:34)."

"I am the Lord, and I do not change (Malachi 3:6)." Scripture contains no contradictions. Every word in scripture is inspired (2 Tim 3:16). Yet the Bible does contain contraries. Note the contrary contained in Jer 31:31-34 as distinguished from Ex 32:34. How do you reconcile God saying He will not forget and eventually punish these people and saying He will choose to forgive and forget? As in all scriptural contraries the reader is required to go deeply for the message. The violation of God's law is sin, 1 John 3:4, and it requires God's justice. Yet the Father's plan enables Him to forgive and forget because of the new covenant that required Christ's emptying Himself (Phil 2:7-8), which resulted in the scales of justice being balanced; and for those who believe in Jesus Christ, their sins forgiven and forgotten.

The word of God is found in the Holy Scriptures, the Bible. The entirety of the Old Testament and the New Testament contains God's word. Whether it is the Pentateuch, Prophets, Chronicles, Kings, accounts of holy people, Proverbs or Psalms, God's word is contained therein. Also the New Testament writing: The Gospels, Acts of the Apostles, Epistles and Revelation all contain God's word. These books in the Bible are not intended to be historical, yet they do have history. The entirety of the recorded Word, the Bible, is inspired; as in 2 Tim. 3:16: "All Scripture is inspired by God and is useful for teaching the truth, and giving instruction for right living, so that the person who serves God may be fully qualified and equipped to do every kind of good." The Gospels depict the historical Jesus Christ and what He said and did, whereas the Epistles depict The Son of God's principles and conclusions, and revelation depicts God's plan through Jesus Christ, The Son of God, from before time to the end of time. The Old Testament carries us from creation through the first Covenant with Noah on through the Covenant of Circumcision with Abraham containing the adventures of the Judges and Kings of God's chosen people, who were guided by God's Law as given to Moses. It concludes with personal experiences of some of the Old Testament heroes, Psalms, Proverbs and the Prophets including Jeremiah who predicted the New Covenant: not one of circumcision but one of Love, Jer. 31:31-34.

"For the truth that Jesus revealed is what inspires the prophets" Rev 19:10. Finally, we reflect on the basic law of nature that all physical creation, including us humans and the stars of the universe experience a birth, life and death. Yet Jesus Christ has predicted in Matt 24:35, "Heaven and earth will pass away, but <u>MY WORDS</u> will never pass away."

This concludes my attempt to articulate that every word in the scripture either directly or indirectly identifies, supports and compliments the Messiah in the Old Testament, and Jesus Christ, the real and only Messiah, in The New Testament, as inspired and authored by the Holy Spirit, as recorded by the prophets, evangelists, Paul and God's chosen writers. Isaiah predicted the arrival of the Messiah, the historical Jesus Christ, who is the Word of God, and John the Baptist (Mt 11:11) became his precursor (Is 40:3-8 & Sirach 49:10).

SCRIPTURE REFERENCES
FOR SUPPORT

Comfort in LONELINESS	Psalm 23 Isaiah 41:10 Hebrews 13:5,6
Comfort in SORROW	2 Corinthians 1:3-5 Romans 8:26-28
Relief in SUFFERING	2 Corinthians 12:8-10 Hebrews 12:3-13
Guidance in DECISION	James 1:5, 6 Proverbs 3:5, 6 Proverbs 16:9
Protection in DANGER	Psalm 91 Psalm 121
Courage in FEAR	Hebrews 13:5, 6 Ephesians 6:10-18 1 John 4:18-19

Peace in TURMOIL	Isaiah 26:3, 4
	Philippians 4:6, 7
Rest in WEARINESS	Matthew 11:28, 29
	Psalm 23
Strength in TEMPTATION	James 1:12-16
	1 Corinthians 10:6-13
	Luke 4:1-13
Warning in INDIFFERENCE	Galatians 5:19-21
	Hebrews 10:26-31
	1 Corinthians 10:12
Confidence in God's FORGIVENESS	Isaiah 1:18
	Jeremiah 31:31-34
	1 John 1:7-9
The Way of SALVATION	John 14:6
	Acts 16:31
	Romans 10:9
	Ephesians 2:8

Printed in the United States
87883LV00002B/1-150/A

9 781591 607267